Praise for Chris Deal &
INCARNATIONS:

"Chris Deal's stories are family secrets, stolen conversations, personal apocalypses, violent acts of desperation, songs to be rediscovered. Sometimes the stories are as big and scary as the dark depths of the ocean and sometimes they are as quiet as whispered regret. Deal fearlessly commits to his vision, so much so, one gets the sense that each and every story in Incarnations represents a hard-earned chunk of Deal's big, dark heart."

—Paul Tremblay, author of *The Little Sleep*

"In the tapestries that Chris Deal weaves, the weight of emotion becomes physical, lands unfurl into the darkness, and hope is dealt in back alleyways like a forbidden drug. Sometimes poetic, sometimes gritty, *Incarnations* is a nesting doll, each layer that much more skin flayed, your bruised heart lurking at the center."

—Richard Thomas, author of *Staring Into the Abyss*

"Like the violent narrative flashes of Brian Evenson or the poetic interludes of Hemingway's *In Our Time*, Chris Deal's new collection summons fever-dream worlds in shades of bright crimson and gunmetal gray. These stories are beauty and terror incarnate. Read them and see."

—Aaron Gwyn, author of *Wynne's War* and *Dog on the Cross*

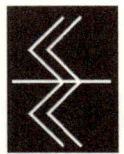

A Broken River Books collection

Broken River Books, 103 Beal Street, Norman, OK 73069

Copyright © 2014 by Chris Deal
Cover art and design copyright © 2013 by Matthew Revert
www.matthewrevert.com
Interior design by J David Osborne

Things Hidden By Leaves first appeared in *Crack the Spine*. *The Song* first appeared in *InfectiveINK*. *In Exile* was originally published in the anthology *Warmed and Bound*. *The Sea of Trees* first appeared in *Twist of Noir*. *Fata Morgana* first appeared in *Bartleby Snopes*. *At Sea* first appeared in *Title Fights*. *Momentum* first appeared in *Outsider Writers Collective*. *Juarez* first appeared in *Underground Voices*. *Let the Bells Ring* first appeared in *Writers' Bloc*. *Cut Through Road* was originally published in the *Southern Gothic Anthology* by PMM P. *Anhedonia* first appeared in *Absent Willow Review*. *Taninim* first appeared in *Outsider Writers Collective*. *Nirvana* was originally published in the *Oprah Read This* anthology. *Incarnation* first appeared in *Rotten Leaves*. *Leviathan* first appeared in *Troubadour 21*. *The Great Schism* first appeared in *The Dead Mule*. *God Use Me as a Hammer* first appeared in *Black Heart Magazine*. *Priest and Pistol* first appeared in *Shotgun Honey*. *Padre Nuestro* was originally published in *In Search of a City: Los Angeles in 1,000 Words* by Thunderdome Press. *A Murder Ballad* was originally published in the anthology *"you're dead and I killed you"* by Brown Paper Publishing. *Where the Water Met the Sky* was originally published in *The Booked. Anthology*. *Morrow* first appeared in *The Zodiac Review*.

ISBN: 978-1-940885-06-3
Printed in the USA.

INCARNATIONS

BROKEN RIVER BOOKS
NORMAN, OK

For my wife.

TABLE OF CONTENTS

THINGS HIDDEN BY LEAVES

The tobacco smoke left her lips and hovered above our table, loose tendrils floating away and mixing in with the greasy offshoot of the kitchen. Smoking had been banned in doors, of course, but when she sat down and asked if she could, the waitress looked around the empty dining room and shrugged. As Pela lit her first cigarette, her lighter scratched and gunmetal with a sickle and hammer engraved, the waitress wedged open the front door. The cook in the back prepared her salad and my BLT as Pela and I sat in comfortable silence.

When the waitress brought the coffee, she had a cigarette ruby-stained along the filter hanging from her empty sausage-skin lips, her hair hanging loose and flat around a prematurely skeletal face. A minute later she brought our food and the waitress's smile strained to reach her bloodshot eyes. The coffee was decent, bland with a hint of possibility. Pela milked every second of her cigarette, holding it to her own lips, her lipstick smeared at the edges. She took measured pulls and carefully blew the smoke to the yellow-tiled ceiling, rolling the stick between her fingers and looking at me with big, wet eyes.

'You want to hit me, don't you?' she said, a smile boiling underneath her lips.

'Mind if I ask you a question?' I took a sip of coffee and swirled the cooling liquid over my tongue.

1

'Why not?' She crushed the cherry against the inner lip of an empty water glass.

'How long exactly have you been fucking my wife?' My question was entirely casual and void of malice.

Pela looked from me to her salad, weighing her words. She speared a cherry tomato on the prongs of her fork and held it up in the clean light where the metal gleamed like a ball of lightning. 'About a year now, I think.' She plopped the tomato between her lips and crushed it like an eyeball between her teeth. 'You were out of town and she went out for a drink. Said she couldn't stand the empty bed, wanted to get away from it for a while.'

'She said that?' My BLT was dry. The waitress had disappeared and the cook looked to be falling asleep on his feet.

'Yeah. You'd been gone for a while at that point, I think, and she needed to get out. She just wanted a drink and that's where we met, at that bar just outside the mall. She was beautiful and fragile and I didn't know she was married. Where were you, anyway?' She folded an entire leaf of lettuce on the end of her fork and stuffed it all in her mouth at once.

'Prison,' I said after three beats of my heart to give the word gravitas, but I couldn't manage it properly. Her eyes went wide for a moment before sliding back into the mask.

'What did you do? Murder? Drug mule? Pederast?' Under the florescent lighting, her skin was yellow and blank, but her cheeks slowly filled with heat.

'I beat a dealer into a coma with a tire iron. He came out of it after a few weeks. Was close to being hit with a murder charge, but they gave me attempted instead.' I took a bite of the BLT. The bread had the consistency of chalk.

'Really?'

'No.'

She deflated, sat back in the booth. I hadn't noticed her move forward. She lit another cigarette. Her hair was obsidian black, her skin pale like a dying moon. When I saw her leaving my house an hour ago, her hair glowing with a greater darkness under the stars and streetlights, I thought she'd as soon gut me as look my way. I put my car into drive and followed after her, the window down. She heard the car and her body stiffened like a board. I pulled up beside her and asked if she knew who I was. She nodded and I told her to get into the car. She complied. We drove in the fading rain to the diner.

'She didn't tell me what you did. Didn't want to talk about you at all, actually. I saw your picture there, the one of you in the middle of a rainstorm. You're not as handsome in person.'

'Trick of the light,' I said.

'I didn't think anything of it, though, but in the morning she started crying. Serious tears, I'm talking about. Like someone killed her puppy. She told me to leave and I did. Might have left my number there for her, though. I'm still hungry.' The smoke was a halo around her head. She took a laminated menu from the rack on the edge of the table beneath the window. A heavy flood of leaves floated on the wind, sticking to my car where it was still wet.

'Try the burgers. They're usually pretty good.'

'You've been here before?' She glanced over her options before motioning to the waitress who had returned from her lapse into nothingness. The cook was face down on the counter, his hands clasped together like he was praying. 'I'll have a double cheeseburger, extra pickles, mayo, and mustard please.'

The waitress didn't write down the order but turned to the cook and called it out. Jerry, that was the cook's name, stood fully up and cracked his back, his neck, before snorting. The waitress asked if we'd like more coffee.

'Might as well leave the pot,' Pela said.

'I have,' I said, before shooting back the final few drops from my cup.

'Hmm?' She killed her smoke and lit another, setting her eyes back dead on me.

'Been here before.' The tiny grounds were like sand clinging to my teeth, my tongue.

'Is this where you planned your horrific crime spree?' Her crooked smile was calculated, artificial.

3

'Yeah, in that booth over by the jukebox,' I said, pointing. She kept her eyes on me, not looking to see that there was no jukebox anywhere in the diner.

'Oh,' she said, her mouth turned to the shape of her word.

'Me and my friend Llewellyn, we knocked over a bodega down off of Central. Our buddy Marcus, a boot camp washout, he was the wheelman. Turns out he couldn't drive stick. Guy thought he knew anything, but the idiot couldn't figure out that clutch. The guy who owned the bodega had the cops on us before we could get a few blocks away. Llewellyn turned on me as soon as he could. I'm guessing a friendship could last forever until a gun's involved. Scored me a Class 5 Felony and a couple years in gen. pop.'

'My god, really?'

'No. You left her crying but she called you back, right?'

'A few days later, yeah. I knew we'd had fun, but I've never left anyone in tears the next morning.'

'Bruise your ego?'

'And my thighs.' She apologized immediately when I flinched, and the way her eyes welled up, she was sincere.

'What'd she say when she called?' The waitress brought over a pot and placed it between the two of us.

'She said she was sorry for what happened. She was married, she said, and had never done that before.' I filled her cup before pouring into mine.

'Cheated?' I took a sip and the coffee was burned, tasted old and bitter and as luscious as manna.

'Yeah, that and been with a woman. She didn't know how she let it happen.' She sneered at her drink. The strength and fury of that look could turn a lump of shit to gold.

'How many drinks did she have?' I reached across the table and took a cigarette from her half-empty pack.

'I think she'd been there for a little while before I noticed her. Maybe three empty wineglasses were at her table when I sat down.' When I placed the smoke between my lips, Pela reached over and lit it for me. It was as if the flame from her lighter held an entire universe that gave way to entropy and died after a moment.

'How many did she have with you there?' I filled my lungs with the delicious burn and the vibrations of every atom in my being slowed to nothing.

'Maybe three more, I'm thinking.' She pulled out one for herself.

'She always was a lightweight, really.'

'You're telling me. Six glasses of wine and she goes home with me.' She exhaled towards the ceiling.

'You're too hard on yourself. I'd have done the same after three.' Jerry's head was against the counter again.

'You've never even thought about sleeping with someone else.' Pela blew a perfect smoke ring.

'I'm a guy, I think about fucking every woman I see.' My own exhalation of smoke, a shapeless mass, passed through the ring and broke it apart.

'Yeah, but you've never thought about really sleeping with someone. Making love, you know, what you and her do together. Real, satisfying sex.' Her tongue peeked between her lips like she was a serpent.

'Again, I think you're being a little hard on yourself.'

'You want to be hard on me, too. Maybe if this were a perfect world, you'd have your chance.' Her leg moved under the table, slipping against my shin.

'Well, that ain't going to happen.' The only way I could get away from her contact was to spread my legs apart.

'Now who's being self-deprecating.' Pela sipped her coffee again but didn't make a face, her eyes sharp against mine, her feet resting on my thighs.

'So, how'd you get her to go home with you?'

'I'm smiled, I flirted, I put my hand on her thigh. I whispered everything I wanted to do to her as my hand slipped oh so slightly higher up. I should have noticed her hesitance.' One of her feet slipped higher, closer to my crotch.

'But she didn't say 'No."' I pushed her feet away before they got too close.

'Nope, and it won't help you if I apologize for that.' Pela sat up straight in her seat, something like a smile playing on her lips.

'It ain't your place to apologize for her.'

'Have you even talked to her about me?'

'She doesn't know I know.' I crushed the cherry between my thumb and forefinger, a tinge of heat dancing over my callused skin.

'How do you know?'

'She was different when I got out. More affectionate. Quieter, too, like she was hiding something, or making up for it.' I dropped the dead smoke in the glass we'd been using as an ashtray and refilled my coffee, then her's.

'For me.' Her voice had grown quiet, hesitant.

'Maybe, I guess, but what happened when she called you back? Did she invite you over?'

'We went for dinner. I guess something of a date. She told me how you were gone, how she was lonely, how she didn't mean for it to happen, that night. Us.'

'But you went home with her again, didn't you?'

'Yeah, but I'm not proud of that.' She ducked her head down low and looked up at me, a near-perfect emulation of sorrow.

'The hell you're not. You're not sorry.'

'To be honest, no.' She started to smile, but caught herself and buried it in her coffee.

'I appreciate your honesty.'

'You're an odd one, you know.'

'Do you love her?'

Her eyes went far away, like she was looking for where the sun would be, obscured as it was by the world. 'I think I do.'

'Does she love you?'

She moved her sight back to my face, her face open now, unsure of what it was I was looking for. 'Ask her.'

'Guess I would.'

'Do you love her? Even after knowing what it is she's done?'

I looked out the window, away from her. The wind had blown hundreds of leaves against my car. It was camouflaged against the empty parking lot, hidden from sight, a car-sized pile of leaves. The pavement was pocked with muddy puddles. The streetlight flickered Halloween orange. The world beyond was as empty as the diner.

'I took some money. That's why I went to jail. I worked in a bank and one of my responsibilities was filling up the ATM. We filled it up with fresh, untainted bills. I don't now if you know this but a new dollar, a whole stack of them, it's remarkably thin. A thousand dollars in twenties is about a quarter-inch thick. You take one or two of them every day for two weeks and it really adds up. You fudge the paperwork, you grease a palm or two, and you could save up one hell of a nest egg. Then you stop. Open up a couple bank accounts and let the money grow for a few years, and you practically have as much money as you stole. Then you turn yourself in, prostrate yourself before the judge for leniency. Pay back what you stole and the bank doesn't know how much that really is. You do a bid, maybe a few more months for bad behavior. You get out, unable to get a proper job, but you and your family isn't wanting no more. The woman you did all that for not even knowing you did it not for greed, but for her.'

'Is that true or are you fucking with me again?'

'It's likely. Plausible, even. A true story at the very least.'

'In that it's a story. I think you're hiding. You've buried yourself under your stories and you're keeping yourself at a distance. You don't let anything touch you.' She traced her forefinger around the edge of her coffee mug and the sound was overwhelmingly absent. 'I'll end it if you ask me.'

'It ain't on me to ask that of you.'

She tried to pay for our meal but I wouldn't hear of it. I left the waitress and the cook a decent tip and dropped Pela off at her car near four in the morning. I'd pocketed the rest of her pack when she wasn't looking and sat out, watching for dawn and killing each smoke, carefully practicing the right twist of the tongue. The sun was in hiding behind a cloudbank when I walked inside. I slipped off all my clothes and slid into bed beside my wife. She curled close to me unconsciously and I wrapped an arm around her, pulling her closer and whispering, 'I know.' She showed no sign of acknowledgement, of consciousness. I did not think of Pela and her and the bed we lay in. I kissed the top of my wife's head and waited.

THE SONG

The old man walked into the coffee shop like a marionette with missing strings. He ordered a cup and sat at a table near the evening's entertainment: a kid fresh out of high school, performing his songs like they were the most important thing in the world. The boy was good. He held the guitar with the care you'd give a newborn child, and sang with a copacetic voice. Most of the patrons went about their conversations without a thought to the music. The old man listened intently as he sipped his drink.

After a routine set of covers songs, the boy played an original, a piece conveying the depth of his soul. The final note rang out but no one noticed or responded, save the old man who clapped earnestly. The boy eased the guitar onto a stand and went outside for a smoke. The old man followed him and bummed a cigarette.

"You're very good."

"Thanks. No one else cares, but thank you." The boy couldn't place the face, but found the old man to be familiar.

"I mean it. You've got talent. Good looking guitar, too."

"It was my grandfather's. The only thing he had to leave when he died."

"It's a beauty. Mind if I give it a play?"

"Why not?" he said as he crushed the cigarette beneath his shoe.

Inside, the man picked up the guitar with a gentle touch, and positioned himself behind the microphone. With a voice like a bell the old man said, "This song was written by the morning star."

Someone out in the crowd coughed. The boy thought the old man was praying for a moment, and then he strummed a chord that rang out through every corner and crevice of the room, catching the ears of all in its path. He hummed a melody that soon gave way to words, each syllable carefully selected and meaningful. The boy found the man's identity hidden in his voice, and was carried back to a memory of his grandfather, who always played one song over and over whenever the boy came to visit, the same song and the same voice that came from the old man.

With an underpinning of chords, the old man sang one final line, "Whether you come from heaven or hell, what does it matter? O Beauty."

The last note faded into a heavy applause that had eluded the boy. The old man handed the guitar back and asked for something to write with. The boy scrambled in his backpack for a notebook and pen, and the old man transcribed the music in full, chord progressions and lyrics.

"It's yours now, the song. Take care of it," the old man said before leaving.

The next week the boy returned to the small stage, and after another set was ignored and dismissed as mere background, he played the old man's song again.

There were tears.

IN EXILE

It was ten years before he saw the sun clearly. For the entirety of that time he remembered those last moments, the warmth flowing down over him as he walked off the bus, wrists and ankles chained and the whole of him connected to the person in front of and behind him. He soaked it in, willing time to slow until the world between heartbeats stretched out past the horizon, memorizing that light and that warmth on his face before it was gone and he was in the dark, the quiet.

They were children together, their parents friends and they became the same. At five they were each other's first kiss, long before they knew what came with such an act. The two ran and held hands, and they smiled, they were always smiling. The girl, her face covered with freckles, would dance and the boy would watch. He'd be quiet for a long time, just observing her. For the girl, dancing couldn't be explained. The movement of her body in time with the music felt right. The boy, he would disappear into himself for long stretches. The days he and the little girl weren't together were days when no words sprang from him; only she could bring them out. He was her audience when she imitated the people in the movies her mother took her to, the plays, and he didn't understand the appeal at first. To him, dancing was just something you did, not something you cared about. Watching her, though, the way she stuck her tongue between her lips as she perfected each move, it'd bring things out from him, words that stayed sacred between them.

The boy's mother went away when he was young and his father became given to long stretches of absence. It infected the boy, the itch for elsewhere crawling behind his eyes. He'd walked out into the woods and find a place to be alone. He smelled the ground like a beast and ate roots until his stomach retched and then he'd walk back inside. When he was older, he'd buy a ticket and show up at the bus station, the idea being he'd leave school behind, his father, the empty house, the hole in the ground, just go away and be forgotten, living on in no one's memories. He once made it four hours away. He stood in the dull corona of a streetlight among the exiles, somewhere outside of nirvana. He bummed a cigarette because he thought it the thing to do and drank coffee that cost a quarter a cup and when it came time to move on, his feet were stuck. He closed his eyes and saw the girl. He bought one more ticket and got home as the sun breached the horizon.

Both knew friendship to be the most fragile of things, and as they moved apart through life, the girl and the boy would remember the other, running through fields and coming home covered in mud, and they would smile, a sacred motion given to no one else. The conversations grew scarce, the boy's words even more so. The girl kept dancing. Practiced and careful, calluses ripped across the balls of her toes. Each movement meant something, the routines told a story she shared with the world. They came to see her dance, people with money and people with love.

She left before him, kissing her mother goodbye and going where she could hone her skills. She did not give him a goodbye, nor did he seek one out. He went to work and each day was the same as those that came before, on and on like an infinity mirror. His eyes grew dull and he thought only of food and shelter. He collected maps of places he had never been and made plans to vanish, but when the day would come, he'd get up early in the morning, have a breakfast of coffee and cigarettes and go to work. When he returned home, he would sit down in his apartment and turn on his television. One night as the world slept on around him, he watched the patterns of static move over the television screen, thinking there to be something important hidden in the chaos. His body went concrete stiff when the blast of virtual snow developed into the thin lines, the crooked nose of his father. The old man's voice took a tight grip on his attention, and the son was offered a job.

The girl made friends fast in her new home, those she trained with. They danced for hours, the same moves and the same routines repeatedly until they were crisp and perfect. She was the best of them, and though some hated her for it, most smiled and asked her for help. She grew stronger in body and mind. Men watched her as she moved down the street, each step holding a world's worth of grace. One day, it was her turn. She was the person everyone came to watch, the person her friends supported, their movements giving agency to her own, and with one last pure pirouette the audience stood and roared her name. Weary but floating, she at first resisted when her friends tried to take her out to celebrate but because of the buzzing in her very being, she relented. At a quiet bar she met a man with a pleasant smile. She woke up in the morning with the elation of the previous night gone, in its place was pain, her face bruised and the man gone. She forgot him and the haze of the night. During the long weeks of practices for her next performance she was off. Her body did not move in the way she expected it to, her muscles were given to more ache. She could feel the dreams she'd held sacred since she was a girl being ripped apart.

He only spoke when someone asked something of him. Conversations were rare and his coworkers thought him an object, less a person, and he was fine with that. Snow came in its time and he liked the clearness of it. He began to think of the large, clean fields as his own mind. He woke one empty day for a drive and found his father in a slovenly motel room on the outer rim of town. The father handed the son a set of keys that belonged to the car he'd last seen his old man drive away in and made him promise to burn it somewhere hidden. He took that junker through the roads out to the low hills beyond town, his momentum carrying him closer to the mountains that loomed like sleeping giants. As the tires hummed over the ice and the slush, there came a sharp curve. Long stretches of emptiness had dulled him, and he turned his eyes to a black bird paused in the middle of a pure, white field. When he looked back to the road, the passenger side tires were veering over the shoulder. A police cruiser was stopped just ahead, the officer hunched over his open trunk. He jerked the wheel but the force of his movement caused the tires to lock up and he kept sliding forward, the weight of his car colliding with the cruiser, pinning the officer between the two vehicles. For a thin moment he thought that this was it, that he would pull back and keep driving, not even going back home for what few objects he cared about. He would empty his bank account and travel south, racing his deed to Mexico where he would tan and learn a new tongue and maybe meet a woman he could hold at night who would remind him in her quiet movements of the first girl. He got out of the car and waited beside the officer, splayed over the hood, as more police traveled fast towards them. The paramedics put the officer into an ambulance and the police, they checked the car's plates and saw there was an alert out for it, for the driver. They asked for permission to search the vehicle and consent was given. Opening the trunk, three officers stood in silence, their eyes trapped, their faces anemic. One turned, gun drawn and finger itching ever closer to the trigger. The son was pinned to the frozen asphalt and saw as they brought a knife, a pair of brown stained jeans too small for any man, out into the open.

He kept his head down in the early days, continuing his practiced silence, and walked through each hour untouched by the informal politics of race revered by the convicted. He fell in with no group, saw no need for protection and became a target. During the slow hours the contained spent idle in the common area an initiate came at him with a straightened mattress spring filed to a harsh point. The initiate thrust and the metal speared deep into his stomach and in his blind efforts of protection he struck the offender twice in the throat. The initiate fell to his knees, blood trickling from the corners of his mouth. He kept his feet and the prisoners began to speak of him as something special.

He received an additional five years onto his sentence. After one more failed attack with batteries buried in toes of a sock and another year, no man attacked him again.

A friend had driven her to the clinic. They sat out in the parking lot for an hour as freezing rain plinked down on the windshield. Tears flowed down the back of her throat and she could not will her legs to take her inside. Dreams and reality were always different beasts. Her company director let her stay on as a teacher and she was able to keep her apartment with the help of her roommate, a fellow dancer. She stood on the side during dance practices, watching and guiding her friends. Sometimes a fear flashed over her that they would soon surpass her. Each day she got bigger and she knew the chance she would go back on stage became slimmer. At night she would rewatch the tape of her performance over and over until every unnoticed mistake became cataclysmic and she knew the applause that came at the end was a joke on her, a series of condescending cheers. Her pillow would dampen and she held the tape in her hands, thinking of ways to destroy it like the forgotten man had done to her. Her mother came to the city and helped her pack her few things before the child was due. They drove back home listening to the wind pushing against the car. Though her mother never asked about the father, she told her everything and the mother smiled sadly and said she would not tell the girl's father. She settled in to her childhood home, getting used to the idea that she was going to be a mother. Before dawn on a Sunday she woke knowing it was time. They drove to the hospital she herself had been born in. Before those long hours she knew pain as something abstract but it became real, a tearing heat from the child working its way out of her.

She sent him letters. Each was written by hand, her calculated cursive holding dreams he didn't want in the hoops of an O. He didn't write back at first. He knew he should have, the world he found himself in. All the old timers spoke of needing an anchor on the outside, even if you are not going to be seeing it again. You needed something to dream about. For most it was a woman, others wanted the stars or a country they'd never been to, offspring or a cold beer. One night in his first year, he woke up to find his cellmate, the

Sacred Heart inked over his chest washed in pale fluorescent light, a sliver of glass shivering in his hand, begging for a word, any word. He relented, if only for a night. He showed his cellmate a picture the girl had sent with a letter. The child was the one he remembered from the years before who had grown into the woman holding her young.

His only peers were the lifers and among the convicts their will was law. His first parole hearing was pushed back to account for the man he left dead in the commons and he thought that was good. His father came to visit and they sat together, both men older than their age, one by a looming death, the other by containment. The father apologized through a breathing tube for the sins that put the son where he now was. The son sat stone still for several long moments, looking over the crags of the old man's face. He forgave his father and it was like a long sigh, the letting go. They hugged, a deed never committed between the two. The father left with a smile. When the old man died in hospice weeks later, the warden looked over the son's record and allowed an excursion to attend the funeral. The son had been inside for a decade of his life. A guard lent the convict a simple black suit and they drove in the prison van out of the gates, the tie tight around his neck, his hands and ankles chained. When they got to the funeral home, the guard asked if he could be trusted to behave himself and he nodded in reply.

A family was gathered in the main hall, their mourning continuing still. An attendant guided the two men into a small room lined with plastic flowers, his father the centerpiece. The old man looked more alive than the last time his son saw him, and the convict stood above the coffin for several long minutes under the guard's watch. He looked down and felt blank, unsure of what it was he should have been experiencing. His mouth was dry, that he knew. His father was small in his repose. The man's uncle came in with his family, an aunt and two cousins he couldn't remember. They shook hands and exchanged forced words. He thought he would like to go back to prison but felt that would not be right, that his presence was as important here as the dead man's. He found a seat and he stared through the world around him, his mind the smooth surface of a lake at midnight. Someone sat in the chair beside him, a woman holding a young child. He looked to her, and she greeted him, her smile breaking through him, and he spoke.

THE SEA OF TREES

The old man swung on the wind not twenty feet into the forest, the rope creaking with his weight as the woods prepared for the night. He had been there for a while, long enough for clumps of hair to have fallen from the dome of the skull, leaving odd patches on the molting, blotted skin. His flesh had started to slip, especially around the noose. The flies and ants had gotten to his eyes and were starting on his tongue, a thick muscle hanging limp from his lips. His shirt had been tucked in but with the pressure from the rope, his waist was exposed, displaying some red and green streaks along the veins where his blood was breaking down. If he didn't have any shoes on, the discoloration would be worse on his feet, as would the swelling. His left foot was hanging back on the log he had used for leverage. The fall hadn't been enough to snap his neck. He'd had to wait for suffocation, and had tried to take things back in his last minutes.

He wasn't even ten days out from the deed, I'd say. Within a week, his chest would rupture from the gases. If his body held out for another two weeks, he'd start to mummify there in the quiet darkness of the trees.

I took the log from below his foot, adjusted it, and stepped up. That close to him, his face swaying near to mine, the smell of him was sickening, heavy with decay and waste. With the weight of his body pulling tight, my blade split the rope quickly, all but cutting the very atoms apart.

He fell into a heap on the ground, his head cracking against the base of the tree he had been hanging from.

It felt wrong to go through his pockets. Even if he was still above ground, it was still grave robbing, but as I took his wallet from his back pocket, I knew he didn't need it anymore. I did. A couple twenties and credit cards with the name Benjamin. They would still be good. His watch was worthless, a cheap plastic imitation of wealth, and I left it on his wrist. He had a set of keys but his car had probably been towed, so that was worthless.

They came from all over to this forest, like it was something romantic to die here. They called it the Sea of Trees, a great forest that stretched along the belly of the mountain, hugging close to the small lake. Every year they found dozens of bodies, some fresh, the rest forgotten in the dark. There were caverns hidden throughout, some known, explored, and others void of the touch of man. The old folk said that ghouls stayed in the deep, coming out only at night for their feasts of the dead. As a boy, my grandmother told me they left the old and infirm to die in the silence of the wood, that some nights specters could be seen wandering in the hell of their deeds, the growth so thick that not even angels or demons could claim them.

Pocketing the money, I put the wallet back and set about pulling him back from the base of the tree, leaving him to be found with some respect before I went deeper into the forest.

Except for the corpses, the woods were untouched by man. Old growth towered, blocking out the sun and wind. Despite the Spring, there was no sign of bird or animal, save the insects attracted by the bodies.

I found the next one fifty feet in. It was a woman, but she was so far gone I couldn't tell her age or what she would have looked like in life. Her sundress was stained with dirt and putrefaction. She was sitting with her back to a tree, a pill bottle still grasped in the bones and muscles that had been her hand. She'd been there for a month at least. She had no pockets or purse, simply a note stuck to her breast. I reached for the slip of paper but stopped before my fingers touched it. It was none of my business why she did what she did.

When I found the third body, it was too late. He was my age, if that. The face still recognizable but he was deep in rigor. As I dug into his pockets, I glanced through the branches to the sky and saw the sun was gone and that night was upon me. Something blind and irrational came over me until I made myself remember I was still close to the edge of the forest. Two hundred steps at the most and I would be back to my car, on my way to buy the evening's meal with Benjamin's money. The young man's wallet was still there, with nothing but his ID inside. Martin.

The last time I'd made the trek, I found an old man with a chest pocked with knife wounds, the blade secure in his hand. He had over a thousand dollars on him and a watch I hocked for twice that. This time, the hunt was barely worth it.

I tossed his wallet onto the ground beside Martin and went back the way I came. The dark had become something tangible, a flood of blackness. Two steps and I tripped over a root. Walking faster, I kept falling. Three hundred paces and the forest gave no sign of letting me go. I turned and ran, stumbling over rocks and bodies, each fall getting me more mixed up. Drowning in the irrational, with every foot I gained, I was more lost. I made a sound like an animal and it was absorbed by the thick nothing of the forest. Not even an echo came back to me. My muscles ached but I kept running, not even in a straight line, zigzagging until my foot found no ground, and the forest swallowed me whole.

FATA MORGANA

My son held my hand as he led me over the hills of dust and down into valleys, past dead streams and carrion bones. There were no words to be had between us. Our journey into the desert was slow. I concentrated on each step, over rock and dry root. After a day's walk, we came to a mesa that offered a full view of the infertile world. I sat in the dirt and he sat beside me. From his bag he took a bladder of water and dried meat and sat them before me. He looked at me like he wanted me to say something but all I gave him was a nod. He stood and turned, but before he left he leaned down and embraced me, his strong arms tight against the frail mess my body had become. This was for the best.

He grew smaller, his body silhouetted against the dying sun until there was nothing left of him and I was alone on the tableland. I pressed myself against the dirt to steal any warmth I could and fell asleep with a rock for a pillow.

A lizard sat perched on my chest when I woke. The sun was still hidden by the earth. I moved slowly to pat the lizard like a pet and it jumped, landing in the dust before running faster than I could imagine. Its tracks, small impressions I had to strain to see, went further into the barrens, away from home. I stood slowly, my bones heavy, and followed the lizard towards nothing.

When the day began, the sun went about its work of beating against the world without care for what there might be down here, I remembered the food and water on the mesa. My mouth was dry and my stomach painfully empty. When I turned around to see if I could make my way back to the mesa, there was no trail for me to follow. I kept forward.

I aimed towards the horizon through the day. It never got any closer. The dust covered me and I was one with the desert.

There was nothing but the dust and the sun and several small blights in the sky. The birds were waiting for me to die. This was for the best.

On the fourth day, my legs and my back were sore and tight, my feet coated with blood and dust, and I could think of no reason to keep walking. I watched the sun rise in the sky from the ground, illuminating the village floating above the desert. I raised my head and watched. It was home. I could make out a figure made small by the village and it was waving to me, calling me back. My son.

My body resisted when I tried to stand up. My arms gave and I fell on my face. After hours of effort I stood on my feet and through many more I took a step. I watched the ground to ensure I would not fall. When I looked back the village in the sky was gone and I was alone.

When I fell I did not get back up. The birds came from the sky and kept me company. This was for the best.

AT SEA

For many years, Nora had an answer at the ready for whenever someone would ask why she was alone, why she always babysat for family and friends instead of having any children of her own, why she lived alone. The answer was always on her lips and floating around her heart. She would say it hundreds of times a day, either aloud to whoever asked or in those silent and evil nights where the time from dusk to dawn stretched on forever. Alone in their bed, she would repeat the answer until sleep would take her away. She had never seen the ocean that her husband left her for.

The men her husband worked for came by the house a year after he left. Large men in gaudy suits, hair cut close to each skull, all perfect in their authority. None of them had an answer for where her husband was. The waters were dangerous. The lifeboat wasn't found. There could be survivors. She pressed her lips tight together and nodded. He could still be alive, they told her, each man the same as the other. One mouth moved in speech and the words come from another's body. She nodded and they left her with a check and a promise for more.

Every year she grew older, her words more rare. Neighbors and sisters would bring their children to her house. A child with brown hair the color of a cornfield in the winter asked why Nora had no husband or children and Nora smiled, her lips losing all severity. "I do have a husband." When the child asked where he was, Nora told her the answer.

Some nights were better than others. On the good ones, she would relive their last night, alone together. The morning would bring separation. He was to board the ship and neither of them would know when they would see the other again. Sleep was an absent thought. They made love fast and slow, desperation propelling each closer to the edge again and again until they couldn't move. As the sun breached the horizon, they were wrapped in each other's arms, memorizing the warmth. When he couldn't stay any longer, he prepared for the day's journey. Before he left, he leaned over the bed she refused to leave and kissed her softly on her lips, lingering, telling her through the contact how much he wanted to stay home, to not ship out, to spend his life in bed beside her.

On the bad nights, she would dream of him, older, skin loose on his bones, in the port of a distant land she would never see. His arms would be around a girl, beautiful in the innocence the dream man was prepared take. He would lean in and lick her in a way he never licked Nora. They would shift to an unlit bedroom and Nora would wake praying not to remember what was seen.

After forty-seven years, a lifetime spent alone, Nora woke and when she opened her eyes, there he was, his hand on hers, his face the same as the day he left. His eyes were not milky like hers, his skin was not blemished or wrinkled. He was as beautiful as the day she vowed herself to him. He smiled and it glowed in the night.

"Where have you been?"

When he replied, it was her words coming from his lips, her answer: "At sea. I was at sea." He leaned down and kissed her, lingering like the last time their lips touched.

Her eyes closed and when she opened them again, she saw the ocean.

MOMENTUM

This started in the early afternoon of Christmas Eve with a car traveling northbound along Highway 77 from the area of Charlotte, North Carolina. Snow was not in the forecast but the roads were still thick with last-minute shoppers and travelers. The car's occupant was chain-smoking cigarillos and doing all he could to remove the weight from his chest. His body was shaking but he did not know why. He had slipped from his familial home and driven, his direction aimed at the mountains past the horizon he could not help but seek out. He had seen the ocean and that was fine, and the Plains States were too flat. He rode the Blue Ridge and the curves, the elevation, the world cracked and angular as if the anger of a quiet god had smashed the landscape into great asymmetrical debris.

As the boy from Charlotte was heading north, the occupant of another car who lived in the general vicinity of the boy's destination had stopped for a celebratory glass of bourbon at the bar he was known to frequent, the holiday all but forgotten as more bourbon and then beer were added to the collection. The man's children had left his home, as had his wife, and the man chose to celebrate every moment he could manage in the manner he found himself. With each drink gone, the boy got closer.

It was after fifty miles spent doing all he could to choke his mind into silence that the boy came to a decision as to

27

what it was he would do. His face grew hot in the bitter wind that dried his tears as he decided he would drive the Blue Ridge Parkway until he found a sufficient overlook, one with a view impossible to replicate and absent of other spectators, and he would stand there for several long minutes with the winter sun falling in the sky and a world of families locked in the illusion of happiness, and he would jump from that overlook and it would be over.

As the boy from Charlotte had made his decision and he crossed over the border from North Carolina to Virginia, the man finished his last shot of bourbon, having moved from a respectable drink to the cheapest the bar had, and he was in the process of paying when the boy took the exit to Fancy Gap, Virginia. From there, the boy would go a few more miles and he would be on the Parkway. When the man stumbled from the bar, the boy was flipping a coin to decide if he were going to continue his momentum north or travel south, back into North Carolina. The coin decided he would be finishing his time in the state he called home. The man turned the ignition and aimed his car in the general direction of his bed, his tires crossing the median and his foot heavy on the gas pedal.

The boy turned into the first overlook he came across but he did not even park, having noticed a large van, coming from the opposite direction as he had been, turn into the second entrance. It had seemed the perfect location. The overlook had a ninety foot drop and was on the inside of a curve on the Parkway, isolated but with an unparalleled view of the mountains further to the south, the valley below. He decided to continue the direction he had been heading, and if a suitable location was not found within a few miles, he would double back and wait until he could follow through with his plan.

As the boy turned back onto the Parkway, the man took the curve far too fast, and in an obscene concussion of shattered glass, buckling metal, shattered bones, profuse bleeding, a rolling impact that came to a sudden, catastrophic silence, the boy's life was saved by the drunken man.

JUAREZ

It was the year of Ana's Quinceanera that she asked her mother for the right to go to work. They had left the crowded bank, the lobby full of police and narcos and small men and women who kept their eyes down and mumbled quietly, their Spanish tinted with indigenous accents, the same as Ana and her mother. The money they deposited had come from Ana's father and brother. The day after Ana's celebration, her brother left to join their father in the wilderness across the border.

You cannot work. You have school.

I can work after. The maquiladoras have shifts from four until eleven.

No.

Their home was too quiet without the men. Though more than the shack they left in Tabasco when Ana was still suckling from her mother, their home now was still less than the house in the pictures her father sent back. Seven rooms rumbling with life. Ana was afraid to take a step in their home, fearful each vibration would shatter the building to nothing.

There are predators here in the city, her mother said. The wolves will tear you apart.

Rosalinda works in a maquiladora. She has for months.

I am not Rosalinda's mother, I'm yours.

If I go to the factory, I can save more money to bring father and brother back.

Hija de tu madre.

Ana hated Ciudad Juarez, hated the fear of dying whenever she left for school. The narcos killed anyone they wanted, even if they had no call for it. When they ate their morning's beans and tortillas, Ana's mother would tell her the news she heard from their neighbor woman whose husband was also up North. Another girl found dead and burned. Beheadings near the border, police and Americans. Ana hated these stories even more than the stories her father and brother sent back. She knew her father was fucking a woman who wasn't her mother. Perhaps her brother had taken to the drink like so many of the other men who went north. She wanted them back, she wanted to leave the city and go home, to their real home.

In the morning, before her class, Ana told her mother that she would be going with her friend, Alona, to study in the library after class. Ana's mother knew that her daughter would be getting on a bus and heading to the dirty streets around the maquiladoras, where she would ask for a job. Ana's mother prayed all night, into the morning, and the next night, but there was no sign from Ana and no letter from her husband. When she went to the payphone she could not get through to him or her son. Ana's mother wanted her men and her girl to come home.

An old man with a face of dust and sun found the girl, prone and open before the uncaring sky. She was twenty feet from the town.

MICTLAN

From the nothing that is the world beyond the city's limits, Xocotl came roaring into existence like a bird from the flames. It started when the dealers out near Cancer Ally started ending up nude of product, their tongues pulled down through their throat in a coyote's grin. Then the fires started in warehouses up and down the river. Guns, with and without badges, roamed the streets with only that name, Xocotl, for a target.

When he struck closest to the seat of power, leaving bodies burnt and torn asunder, there came a survivor. His eyes had been plucked from their sockets and found in a glass of scorpion wine. His voice was made of velvet, the amaurotic witness said, and the shape of his form was that of a jackal.

When the city's Jefe, an old man with blood on his shoes, found the egg on his door step, crushed beneath an absent boot, he knew the day of his life was closing in on sunset. He consolidated what men he had that maintained the loyalty he required in his home, waiting for the man they called Xocotl to come for him.

Each creak of wood was an enemy blade slipping through the shadows. Each night held little promise of morning. The Jefe waited for his death while the streets were free for the taking. Product flowed once again, bodies sat unclaimed in the morgue. An egg hatched out in the nothing and the city was claimed.

LET THE BELLS RING

The streets were a thick sheet of soiled, blackened snow, thick with week-old ice that kept all but the defiant or desolate of souls at bay in their homes. A lone halogen bulb illuminated Frayer Street, casting the tainted downfall in a halo above his head. The sun had been hidden for days behind clouds hanging heavy like ash in the sky, and was hidden now by the world beneath his feet. Every passing minute brought the temperature closer to zero. Morris walked slowly, picking his way with careful steps over the hard drifts along the sidewalk. The glacial currents seeped through his bones, weighing him down more than the waning days of his epoch. His lungs burned with the exertion that cast him towards his destination. A sentence tried to work its way up his throat but he choked it down to his bowels. No words were allowed to escape his lips. He spoke only through his movements, the motion of his decaying husk, the obscured and paling light that fled his eyes. The blood he once spilled for a righteous anger was cooling under his paper skin. The lone spark of need in his body fueled his agitation forward. His aim and his path was the extent of the world, all else was abyss and void. Morris was alone in the nothing, and that was more atrocious than his assured annihilation. His cautious steps took him through the dead city, from the home he had claimed for the reign of years through to the border that he had passed only once in his life, as if it were a fire to be crossed in the most trying of times. The time before was the result of a conflagration across the sea. This was for the inferno in his soul. The garden of stone was where it had been since he was a boy. A gathering place for dust below the archaic belfry. His end was among the rows, there with the most recent crop. He brushed away the accumulation on the stone that bore her name and stood there above it, above her, the words fighting against their way from the vault where he kept them, a struggle he was quickly losing. Words were bitter on his tongue since he brought her here to the garden. He was a statue there, in the obscene glow of the snow, until the hour struck and the bell in its tower rang, the sound filling the wold with the fury of the unseen, echoing off every falling flake, touching every sleeping soul for miles. The violence of the tone broke those words loose from his body, and he could only hope they would reach her beneath the dirt.

CUT
THROUGH ROAD

I met Lloyd in 1972. Was not long after my Daddy died. Momma said it was a heart attack that took him, that he was walking up to the Pucket's store and died halfway there. He'd fell down on the side of Cut Through Road. When I walked that road that they'd cut through a tobacco field I could always find a warm breeze blowing through, even then near the end of summer before they brought in the plants.

I was walking along the same road when I was stopped by a couple of white men in a knocked up truck. They pulled up beside me and got out, a taller boy with bright red hair and a shorter, blond one. The blond one didn't have no shirt on and had a drawing on his arm of a naked lady. The tall boy had a knife and told me to give him my money.

I said I needed it for a biscuit. I walked up to Pucket's about once a day except for Sundays for a jelly biscuit and a Coke but that tall boy just told me to give him my money.

They came close and the blond one took my hand in his and twisted it up beyond my back and it hurt. The tall boy put that knife to my belly and said he weren't going to ask again.

About then a blue truck pulled up behind theirs and a man came out holding a baseball bat and he was yelling for them to get away from me and some words my Momma told me not to say. The blond one let go of me and the tall boy turned that knife to the man.

He had light brown hair cut short and he was strong looking, taller than that blond one but shorter than the redhead. He took that bat and swung at the knife and that tall boy his hand went limp and the knife went out into the tobacco field the road cut through and that boy started yelling when that bat hit the other on the jaw and he spat blood and went to the ground. The tall boy went to turn and run but that bat got him in the side and he went to his knees and the bat got him on the head and he was quiet and not yelling no more.

You alright, the brown haired man asked, and I said yes, sir.

You don't have to call me sir, he said.

My Daddy always said to say sir, I said, and he said your Daddy sounds like a smart man.

Yes, sir, he was, I said.

He asked my name and I told him and he said hello, Frank, I'm Lloyd.

I guess by then he seen how I was. He asked me if I knew how to keep a secret and I said it was the least I could do. He said something about those boy's plates, how it didn't look like no one around there would miss them.

We stood there a bit, him breathing heavy like my Daddy used to do and wiping his forehead with his hand and me not knowing what to do. I was hot and hungry and wanted to go get a biscuit and go home to Momma.

Where were you going? he finally asked. I told him Pucket's store and he thought on it and reached to his back pocket for his wallet. He pulled out a couple of bills, bigger one's than I'd seen. I get checks from the government but my Momma always took care of those and would give me money for Pucket's but never bills as big as those.

I was heading that way myself he said. If you could do me kindly and pick me up a loaf of bread and some eggs you could keep what's left. I'll take care of those two and give you a ride home. I said that sounded about right.

I walked on like I'd been, only with more money, thinking over and over to myself bread and eggs. At Pucket's the owner Ronnie helped me out like usual, not saying nothing about the big bills I handed him. He just slipped one back over the counter to me and pressed a couple of buttons on the register and changed the big bill out for smaller ones and handed them to me and wished me a good day. Ronnie was always a good fellow, especially for a white man. He and my Daddy were always good friends, so I always liked him. I said thank you, sir and got the bag and my coke and left. Outside I nodded to a white man who was getting gas and he said nothing back as I started for home.

Around when I got to where those boys had stopped me I saw their truck was gone, as were they. I kept on walking when the blue truck pulled up beside me. Hey, Frank, he called from the open window. He asked if I wanted that ride and I told him sure.

He leaned over and opened the door. I got my biscuit wrapped in grease paper from the bag and handed him the rest and got in. To me, it was a nice pickup but I'm sure few else would have thought it.

I pointed the short ways home and we talked for a bit about nothing much. He did not ask again if I could keep a secret and I did not ask if he'd killed before. My Momma had told me about the war and how a lot of boys had to hurt people over there to keep from being hurt themselves. He seemed to me different from the folk I knew. He reminded me a bit of my Granddaddy who'd been over in France during the second big war, the way their backs were straight always, the respectful manner they talked to everyone. I'd ask Lloyd sometime later about it and he thought a moment and told me about some of the things he'd done over there but not too much to scare me. I never was scared of him though.

He pulled up to the house my Granddaddy had built when he'd gotten home from France and I had about forgot about the money left over from what he'd given me. I knew he'd said to keep it but I didn't know if he really meant it. When I pulled it from my pocket he just waved it away and said a promise is a promise and that I deserved it. When he pulled away I thought it'd be the last I'd see of him.

Three days later I'd walked up to Pucket's for my jelly biscuit and a Coke. Sitting out front when I went to walk home were a couple of old white men and then that blue truck pulled up to the pumps and Lloyd came out and waved at me. One white man, a bald one called Tunny, turned to the other named Curt and said Curt do you know what's worst than a nigger?

Can't quite say I knows what, he responded.

A retarded nigger and they both laughed hard at it. My Momma told me never to listen to those who said things like that. They was worst off than me by a lot she'd say. I was about to walk home when I saw Lloyd walk over to them and lean down close to their faces and he whispered something and they went pale and when he stood up I thought I saw him put something shiny back into his pants pocket.

Do we have an understanding he said and they nodded and he went in and paid for his gas and when he came back out they were still there, quiet and doing all they could to avoid looking me in the eyes. He asked if I wanted a ride and I said sure.

In his truck he asked I ever played checkers. My Daddy used to play with me and my brother when we were kids but not much since, I told him.

We should play some, then, he said. He drove back to his house, an old cabin a couple of miles from my home. It had electricity and water but not much else. The cabin had a kitchen and bedroom that were not separated and a bathroom. There was a table by the fireplace where he set up the checkerboard. Want to be red or black, he asked. I said, Red.

We played for a couple hours, him winning mostly but I had some good games. During the play we talked a little, getting to know each other as friends do. He told me about the war and I told him about what it was like growing up with my condition. He went quiet when I asked him what he did. After a few minutes and he asked to be kinged, he said he stole things. I didn't ask anymore.

When he drove me home he said I like you and I thought that was funny. He said I reminded him of himself only as a better person. After that he said he couldn't stay in town much longer. He had to take care of things with his father. He asked if I liked his cabin and I said it was nice. If I wanted, he said, I could use it if I needed. He dropped me off at home and we said goodbye and that was the last I saw of him.

The next day I went up to Pucket's and went to pay and Ronnie said it was taken care of. I had a tab and anything I needed would be taken care of. Those two old white men, Tunny and Curt were there but they didn't say a thing to me.

Sometime later, my Momma went to bed one night and didn't get up in the morning. I called my brother Jimmy and he came down from the city and helped take care of matters. He asked if I wanted to stay there in my Granddaddy's home but I knew I could not take care of it like my Momma and Daddy had.

Jimmy had done good for himself and had a family in the city and asked if I wanted to come live with them but I didn't want to intrude on their lives. I told him about the cabin and he and I went to look at it and he asked the landlord who said the place wasn't his. Someone named Copper had paid for it and kept up on the taxes. He had a letter from the man for me. It was from Lloyd, saying the cabin was mine as long as I wanted it and to take good care of it. Jimmy helped me move in and he took care of my parent's home, not wanting it to leave the family.

The night I moved in it was cold and I wanted to start a fire. The tobacco was still up but it'd been getting cold at night. There were some old logs out back and I brought them in and put them in the fireplace but when I pushed them towards the back, three of the bricks fell out and behind them was a package wrapped in old newspaper sitting in the hole. I was close to tears when I opened it. Several stacks of old twenty dollar bills with a note from Lloyd that said to use the money but not too much, as some folks were looking for it.

The cabin was further from Pucket's than I was able to walk, so I used a small bit of that money to buy a bicycle from a neighbor. I hadn't much need for it, as my Momma had Jimmy help set up a trust fund for me, using the money she'd saved from her own work and what I got from the government. I needed to pay some utilities but that was it. With the bicycle I started going to the library and about once a week or so Jimmy and his wife would bring me to their home for dinner. That tab Lloyd had gotten me for Pucket's was still good and for once in my life I was living on my own, something Momma had said she doubted I'd be able to do but I think I would manage decently.

I took that bicycle down to Pucket's about a year after Lloyd left and as I was drinking my Coke I heard Ronnie and some men talking. They found an old truck deep in the woods out on the outskirts of the town with a couple of skeletons in it. They figured those guys were two crooks who'd been riding through and had gotten drunk and crashed into a big tree the truck was wrapped around and that was the last I heard of those two. Ronnie rang me up and put my stuff on the tab and wished me a good day and I said thank you, sir.

Sometime after I bought that bicycle I got a knock on the door early one Saturday morning. There was a man in a nice suit there who said he was from the FBI and wanted to ask me a few questions. I asked him to come on in and offered him some tea but he said no, thank you. I asked him what I could help him with and he asked if I ever knew a fellow named Dan Cooper and I said honestly, I didn't.

He held up an old twenty dollar bill and asked where I got that from and I guess it was one of those I bought the bicycle with and told him someone I knew a while back gave it to me. The FBI man asked for his name. I told him Lloyd and he asked if I knew his last name and I told him I didn't. He asked when was the last time I saw this man and I said it's been a year or so. He thought on it and I guess he knew that was all he'd be able to get from someone like me.

As he left he handed me a slip of paper with his number on it if I knew anything about where he could find the man. I told him yes sir, I would and he nodded and when he left I threw that piece of paper in the trash. I knew exactly where Lloyd or whatever that man called him was. On that letter he'd left with the former landlord he'd put his address. I even wrote him and told him about the FBI man and he wrote back asking why I hadn't told the man anything. When I wrote I told him that he was one of the few people who never called me nigger or retard or faggot and that he was my friend. When he wrote back all he said was thank you.

ANHENDONIA

It stood there for hours, not swaying with the beat of a heart, with no aching muscles, no pain, nothing. It just stood there, giving no mind to the cold, no thoughts to the ruined apartment, the soiled carpet or the obscene streaks and handprints on the walls. It watched the open window, the world outside, watching with static eyes. The only movement in the apartment was the snow and ash brought in on the wind, the only sound an unending series of barks from the floor above. When the dog started, the thing wandered about, making foul, preternatural sounds, guttural snarls and reverberations discordant and counter to the shape they originated from.

The power went out three days back, taking the heat with it. Snow had been falling like bird shit for weeks, off and on, mixing with the ash from the fires consuming the surrounding neighborhoods. They hadn't reached the complex yet, though. It was so cold, I kind of wished they would. When I was a kid, there was an electrical fire one night in my family's trailer. The warmth, like the devil's breath on my cheek, was comforting in my sleep before my dad kicked in my door and took me in his arms, outside to the bitter cold. I've never been as content, as cozy as that night. Sometimes, late at night with the fever in full swing,

I prayed the fires would rage into the complex, taking those things and me with it.

The fever was getting worse. It wouldn't break, no matter what. Even without the heat, I was managing a good sweat. Still, even with the sweatpants underneath the robe and the blanket I'd taken to wearing like a death shroud, I couldn't get warm.

The kitchen had gotten bare. Starting in the fridge, when power went out, I ate all the leftover takeout, even the Chinese food that was of questionable age. The second day I ate the vegetables, even the raw ones. I thawed various packages of peas, carrots, broccoli, and even with a full stomach, I was more and more unfulfilled. Boredom, it could have been. I tried improvising for a warm meal, filling the sink with paper, books, anything burnable I could find, putting the food in a pot, but it couldn't get hot enough, or for long enough.

I'd kill for a cup of coffee, for a damn steak.

Despite the temperature and the fever that started almost as soon as that thing bit me, not hard or deep, but breaking the skin, I was spending the majority of the time out on the balcony, sitting on a lawn chair, watching my breath float out into the nothing. Across the street from my apartment someone else had the same thought, to bunker down until something, anything changed. Her name was Sarah, she had yelled across the cavernous fifty feet separating us. I told her my name was Ben. I noticed her there the same day I pushed the couch against the door, locking myself in. We talked until we were hoarse, about whatever came to mind, anything to break up the monotony of waiting. I'd seen her before, of course. I'd see her walking her German shepherd every night after she got home from work. Never did talk to her, of course, not until we were the last people in the area. Couldn't remember ever seeing a car in her extra parking spot, never saw someone leaving her at the door after a date, hoping for the invitation inside.

With nothing but time, because it was too cold for Sarah to be out on her balcony for long, I tried to read. I tried a couple magazines, but I couldn't even pretend they held my interest, not even the few I had with what was considered erotic pictures of women in various levels of clothes. There wasn't a point. I tried some of the books I had collected but never gotten too, literary masterpieces I hadn't had time for. *Moby Dick* was pointless, same with *Gravity's Rainbow*. I didn't even have the patience for a page of *Finnegans Wake*. I got a couple chapters into *One Hundred Years of Solitude*, and I remembered loving everything about it years before, but I threw it against the wall. I screamed just to make a noise, to hear something, to excise the frustration, the isolation. Those things heard, and they tried again to get to me, the shuffling, the weird sounds, like animals locked in cages. Sarah, if she heard me, she said nothing about it.

She had a survivalist radio, one of those that you have to wind up for power. All the stations were off, the only thing she could hear was a constant emergency broadcast, informing us the power would be restored soon, that the best thing to do was wait in home. Don't open the door for anyone, it said, except for police or military. They were sweeping the area for survivors, and any found would be taken down to the National Guard armory in south Charlotte. They announced three days back they would be working through Huntersville, but we never saw anyone. The message had remained the same since.

Those things were still in the area, and every time I looked down from my second floor apartment, there was at least one wandering around, occasionally looking up at me, something like hunger hanging on its cadaverous face. I was getting to look more and more like those things with every glance in the bathroom mirror.

The thing, the abomination, had been a statue for hours, days maybe, in the winter chill. Time was nothing, the cold of no consequence. It stood there, waiting for something, anything. Outside, it's ilk staggered through the snow, looking for their antithesis, a goal unknown even to them, to the thing standing still in its former apartment. It had clawed and moved as fast as it was able among the rooms when the dog started barking, trying to get to the direction the sound came from. It reacted with the stimulus. It needed sound, movement, something to strive for, the purpose of the pursuit a remote instinct, almost alien. Then came a sound, different, foreign to ears it should have been known to. Resonant even across the parking lot, the sound pierced through the silence, above the yapping, starving dog. The thing shifted, muscles tightened and loosened.

"Do you have family around here?" I asked her, the first time we spoke, the day after I locked myself in, the day the fever started.

"No. They're up in Ashville."

"That's a nice area." It felt weird, having such a simple conversation by yelling.

"Yeah."

"Why'd you come down here?"

"For work. I'm an assistant professor at the university."

"What do you teach?"

"English. Creative writing."

"Are you a poet?"

"Somewhat. I can teach kids how to write poetry, but I can hardly put together a stanza myself."

"You'll get there."

"I hope. What do you do?"

I wanted to lie. I'm a VP at one of the banks. A doctor. "I work in retail."

"Where at?" She didn't even skip a beat.

"In the Village."

"How is that?"

"Decent enough."

"I'm going to get some sleep," she yelled, and with a soft smile I couldn't return, she was gone.

The fever would not break. Sleep was harder and harder to come by. I would lie in bed for hours, hoping for a nod, wanting nothing at all but the release of nothing, from nothing. The days were getting longer, the conversations with Sarah the only thing to look forward to. There was some food left, but I couldn't bring myself to eat. The books had been burnt in the sink for illusory warmth. I stayed in bed until I heard her call to me, then I would rise and go to the safety I felt by simply seeing her, the most unobtainable woman in the world.

I tried to sleep, to dream, hoping for a REM state, those firing neurons in my head to give me some time away from the purgatory of this place. Five nights after the internment, I laid down against futile hope for the annihilation of sleep. I dreamed I stood in the familiar landscape of my childhood home, the backyard. I didn't know where my family was, nor any of the various dogs of my youth. I was beside the old shack my dad had used as storage. Inside, home to any number of vermin were enough broke car parts to build an astoundingly bizarre automobile.

The world around me was the same as it ever was, but there was a particular turn in the wind and the sky was a shade never seen on this rock, the clouds pulsing and shifting, black as the dead of space, with violent undercurrents threatening to erupt the evening sky above me like something out of the apocalyptic ravings of a mad prophet, and then there came a fury and the currents of clouds became a vortex, bright as the sun, a swirling of fire high above the ground and from that malevolent tourbillion came the roar of a dying god. There came a rupture in the sky and a wave of holocaust turned the air and the land to char and I could feel it blistering me and then it was gone, only a trail in the air left by the conflagration, and like any great storm it could have only been the eye. The ambiance was ripped apart in a great searing flash and the very atoms of my being were torn away into the furor as I lifted a futile hand to protect myself and then there was nothing but the black expanse of eternity, and that was the end.

There was a flogging and an ataxia of limbs under the blankets, a body expiring, and entropy was winning the struggle, the battle nearing completion. Beneath his eyelids there was chaos, an apocalypse unfurling in his most vulnerable aspect. The lungs struggled in their mission, breath stertorous and ragged, coming faster and faster until a final climax, an exhalation, and the form was vacant.

The body inert, prostrate on the rumpled bed, blankets and sheets sodden with sweat and waste, the smell of no consequence to anyone. Pallor spread across the skin and the blood pooled in the extremities, the body as cool as the room, the world outside.

The prone form lay decumbent, its rest unceasing, the entire room devoid of that bizarre spark of being, the only movement the currents of air from the open balcony door, snow and ash thrown about in cryptic patterns, alien tongues where a meaning could be found if there were any eyes there to observe them.

In the land outside the improvised sepulcher, the deviant, unnatural beasts roamed in search of sustenance, of prey, and not more than fifty feet from where the man lay in elegiac slumber, another body was mirrored in languor, the woman dreaming of a life before decimation, of a man who could have been anyone but represented the inaccessible soul currently on decomposition's door.

Her body twitched, and the waking world imposed on the nirvana of sleep. She stretched and sighed, her voice harmonious in the hush. Leaving her bed, she went to the bathroom, dipping a hand into the bathtub full of water. As soon as she lock herself into her abode, she had filled the tub, the sink, unsure of how long she would be trapped, ensuring survival in the only way she could.

Sitting on the edge of the bathtub, her thoughts went to where she strove to keep them, the cacophony the world had turned to, the gun her father had given as a gift when she left the familial home, an instrument of protection whose mission could so easily be corrupted and perverted. The weapon sat loaded on her bedside table. She moved her mind from the suicidal urges and envisioned the man she knew so little about, over the crowd of things, whose face was now the only thing that kept her from the horrific deed.

Across the cavernous distance, there was an unnatural twitch of cadaverous flesh, an execrable motion as fingers flexed and jaw clenched. The thing that had once been a man sat up in its soiled clothes. To its feet, it unknowingly tested its capability to hold position, upright, tendons and tissue straining with the anomalous act.

In an imitation of its former behavior, the thing put a foot before the other, then repeated the movement, locomotion obtainable, it went from the bedroom to the erstwhile living room, and with obscene, and with vacant and glazed eyes, it took in the space it occupied. With elephantine drive, it went towards the barricaded door, hitting the coffee table and knocking several glasses to the floor where they shattered with a startling noise, disturbing the serenity, causing the dog left in the abode above to stir, to howl.

The counterfeit life was driven into action, trying to get to the animal, for a purpose only hinted at. The simulacrum was a void in comparison to its previous existence, nothing stirred in the blank of its mind, but the motion was real, the thing was no lie, and the noise of the animal gave it intent, and it threw its limbs against the obstructing couch, unable to reach the exit, to get approach the life it needed to extinguish. In its deranged rampage, the matter the thing had excreted in death was strewn around the room, on the walls, the useless furniture.

Unable to accomplish the only point to its being, the insulting brute suspended movement, and stood in the living room, the wind and the snow blowing against its repellant body, and the beast waited with the patience only afforded to the dead.

"Ben," she yelled across the divide, above the beasts below. Sarah refused to look down at them, to see how many were there. She knew she should not ignore them, but could not see them again. She called out again, and again. She needed him to respond. Five days trapped in the room. Her cellphone still had power, but there was no way to call out. The towers were down. She could still dial 911, but had given up after the second day without an answer. She called for him again, to say anything, to be there, even if he was what could have been across the world, she could see him, could talk to him, but he wasn't answering. A tear fell, almost freezing against her cheek. She went inside, went to her bed, and laid down. There was nothing else to do.

It watched from the dark room, eyes dead and uncaring, but the unnatural drive that animated the form was screaming like the dead of Hell, and though there should be nothing there, the nerves of its being like dead circuitry, allowing none of the electrical impulses of life to animate the construction, it was standing with atrophied legs, it was watching with blank eyes, and the abominable drive forged in the nothing of dead brought the atrocious essence to the fore in a gnashing of teeth, in an abhorrent, animalistic growl, in languishing muscles that strove for the sound, the impetus that forced it out the balcony door, over the railing, down ten feet to the dead grass below.

The impact was of no consequence, and it was crawling towards the direction the voice came from. Its progress too slow, it rose to its feet, one deliberate step after another, pushing its kind away if those foul progeny came between it and its destination. Every despicable being had heard the calls, and they each made for the woman, isolated as she was, cut off, thinking herself safe.

Asleep in her bed and her denial, she had idea the crowd that had formed at her balcony, a gallery of maleficent admirers, and though some, perhaps bored of the interim, wandered away, towards anything that could capture their attention, the thing that had been Ben was secure in its attraction, its base appetite, and though the throng was halted at the sight of the balcony's banister, it stood there for only a moment, knowing peculiarly its goal was further, that patience was a worthless virtue.

It went to the wall of the ground floor, and started pacing, back and forth, seeing the obstacle and though there was nothing in it that affected consciousness or thought, it found its way to the glass door of Sarah's downstairs neighbor. The closeness overcame the difficulty, and the dreadful anatomy was cast against the barrier, repeatedly, torso and head and shoulders slammed against the glass until there was a crack, then a shattering, and despite the piercing of the body, the complete lack of blood save a draining of residual viscosity, the thing was inside the building, closer to its innate objective.

The building was silent, still. There came, through connecting air-conditioning ducts, through the very walls and floors, the sound of a sob, scarcely audible, but there, and it drove him forward like a shark at the hint of blood, the passion spurring the thing forward, towards the open apartment door, giving not thought for the people who had made the chambers home. The sound came clearer from the stairwell, and the fiend followed the sob like a scent, up, over steps, turning with the path of the stairs, and then the thing was outside the door, a few inches of wood separating it and what it needed, the aberrant goal.

It thrashed against the door, repeating the initial act of entrance, again and again and again, but the aperture showed no sign of give. The sobs from the inside grew louder, and the thing threw itself against the entryway harder, and the beast's kin were trickling into the building at the growing fury, despite the sudden culmination, termination of the woman's cries.

More bodies were beating against the entrance, the need overcoming the apathy of the dead.

POWDER

Penny slid into the bedroom, a shadow hidden in a greater darkness. She stood on the balls of her feet, concentrating her weight. A passing car cut a shard of light through the night, illuminating the sleep form on his side of the bed, his body curled onto its side, facing the empty window, away from where she slept. In the kitchen, dirty plates and takeout boxes. In the living room, a newspaper devastated and strewn like viscera over the couch and coffee table. An abhorrent series of nickel-sized depressions, three large and one small mark less than an inch apart, gouged into the drywall that marked the path toward the bedroom, a trail of powder tinted red. His breathing slow and constant as it could only be for the unconscious, a heavy constant in the stillness of the apartment.

The world turned slowly closer to dawn. Penny closed her eyes and he was her ocean, the sound of him, the memory of his warmth washing over her. She hid her bag in the closet and removed each article of clothing like it was a ritual and folded them carefully into their place amongst his. Like a shadow she moved to the bed, sliding over the cool sheets to fill in the gap where she belong. Pressing against his back, she folded her legs to fit perfectly behind his. He moved as only the sleeping can backwards, closer, as she put a hand over his chest and felt the heart beating there through muscle, skin, and bone. She touched her lips to the base of his neck and felt the sparks forming at the edges of her eyes.

The warmth of the world came from him, the sun burned deep inside and he was its avatar. Penny thought of the tears, understood them intellectually but without anything baser, keeping the causes locked away where she could hope to forget them. Penny formed the image of his lips bruised with hers and smiled into his skin, thought of the time her teeth pressed too deep and how his essense tasted of her namesake, how she swallowed him that night and never wanted him gone. His face was hidden, his voice absent. Would he show more sign of anger or mirror her tears? She didn't know if his voice, when she found it and drawed it out like an abused animal, would be raspy or broken from screams. His knuckles were swollen and she traced them with her finger a feather. Over the first two were spots coagulated blood and torn skin. His hand moved her's to his lips and she broke.

'You smell of gun powder.'

TANINIM

When the Reverend Tom Ward stepped to the pulpit, the congregation knew there was something off. In his right hand there was a lowball glass, despite his adamancy that neither food nor drink was allowed in the sanctuary. His suit, the Sunday best as he would say, was absent. He wasn't even wearing his collar. The Reverend was wearing dusty black pants and a wrinkled white button-up with stains under the arms the color of a career smoker's teeth. His drink had spilled down his front several times. His hair, all but immaculate on most Sundays, was greasy and jetting out in Byzantine patterns, the brown spotted with newly discovered gray, matching the three days of growth on his chin. His eyes were harrowed and haloed with spider webs of burst capillaries.

None of the Church Elders had the immediate sight to leave their seats out with the congregation and escort the Reverend off the pulpit until he was well underway with what would have become his greatest sermon.

It wasn't until he said, "And La Malinche is seen in contradictory terms even today, much like those motherfuckers the Yankees, the Judas Steinbrenner, who betray the sanctity of the sport like some say La Malinche betrayed Mexico, and I can walk right outside these doors to the parking lot and I promise you I will count no less than twenty Yankee stickers on the back of your cars, but of course, we must remember him, Steinbrenner, for the success he had, much like we must remember La Malinche for instigating a new age in Mexico, for good or ill, who but our dear Lord can say. This in mind, should we not then thank Judas for what he did for us, the Christian of today, in betraying Yeshua bin Yosef, or Issa, as our Islamic brethren know him, should we not thank Judas Iscariot, the man of Kerioth, for if he did not betray Issa, would we be here today? Would we be fucking Christians at all?"

Elder Jones managed to get the power cut to Ward's microphone before he went any further. Elder Mitchell quickly took the stage and escorted the Reverend from the pulpit to his office while Jones addressed the congregation, telling them that the service was to be ended early today and to go with the grace of God. The Elders forced a cup of coffee into Ward's hand and locked him in his office while they convened just outside his door. After a few moments, the blues could be heard coming from the office. Ward was a fan of Robert Johnson, and he was singing along, off-key, but with a joyful voice.

It took no great effort to decide that Tom Ward's time as Reverend had come to an end. It was decided that Michael Peterson, the Reverend's second in command would take control. He was in charge of the Bible studies, was well-liked, respected, and the obvious choice. Elder Buchanan was sent out into the flock to bring Peterson before the Presbytery. The great mass of the congregation was still in their seats, concerned and confused at what they had seen. Certain members of the laity were talking in hushed, disparaging terms of their Reverend and how they had seen this coming, a lie each knew and accepted. The Elders discussed with Peterson the decision and he was more than happy to take the role.

Elder Jones, being a man of some respect among the Elders, relayed the order to them and the new Reverend to get the affairs of the church in order before he entered the office of the now former Reverend Ward, who was sitting behind his desk for what would prove to be the final time, looking out the window to the parking lot, an open bottle of bourbon on the desk, and a cigarette hanging from his thin lips. Elder Jones turned off the stereo on the bookshelf and sat in the chair before Ward.

"You're not allowed to smoke in here," Jones said after a moment. Ward made a sound that could have been either a chuckle or a cough, but said nothing coherent. "What the hell, Ward?"

"Moctezuma Xocoyotzin, heir of Auitzotl, that man, he— he must have known his time had come," Ward said.

"What?"

"He stood, he stood there before his people, asking them to relent and they cast their stones at him. Sound familiar?"

"The hell is wrong with you?"

Ward laughed like an asthmatic before continuing. "No longer the honored young one they had praised him as, Moctezuma wished to spare his people anymore suffering. The years, they had foreseen many omens, many signs that the cycle they were in, well, would be the last. No culture can last forever, they knew that. Everyone has to figure that out. The end always comes."

"We've decided that Michael Peterson will be taking over as Reverend, effective immediately. He was the obvious choice."

"Every generation has the fear that theirs would be the last, but to face the approaching doom, to see the feathered-serpent Quetzalcoatl in human form, shit, that's got to be unprecedented, to make the— the doomsday prophecy, and that damn thing comes true. He, um, Moctezuma, he sent two ambassadors to the Yucatan to greet the newly arrived god. When he learned that Quetzalcoatl was approaching with an army, he— he sent more gifts to appease the— the apparently angry god. When the serpent massacred the people of the sacred Cholula, Moctezuma, shit, he must have known what would come next. Once Quetzalcoatl arrived in Tenochtitlán, he offered flowers from his own garden and submitted his throne.

"When Quetzalcoatl saw the sacrifices of the temple, and was offended, Moctezuma immediately had the temple cleaned and allowed Quetzalcoatl to install icons of his own god, odd of a concept as that may be, a god who worships a greater deity. Moctezuma and his people had betrayed Quetzalcoatl by allowing men and women to be slain, something the feathered-serpent god had opposed for generations. When Quetzalcoatl left Tenochtitlán in the control of an emissary, Moctezuma, well, he submitted to him as well. The priest of a god was to be as honored as the god himself.

"When— when the priest saw the celebrations in the great temple, he had the upper classes butchered. When the people of Tenochtitlán had enough of these massacres, they rose up to the authority of the god, and Quetzalcoatl's emissary took Moctezuma captive, threatening his very fucking soul if the chaos didn't come to an end.

"So— so it was that Moctezuma stood before his people and knew his legacy was tarnished. It's funny that, just before he was strangled by a lowly soldier of Quetzalcoatl, Moctezuma was worried more about his legacy than the fate of his people. He had been Motecuhzoma Xocoyotzin, the honored young one. Now, he was nothing but a victim of his god. From the sea had come a great leviathan, and from the sea had come the end."

"Very enlightening."

"Was it a good sermon?"

"What?"

"My sermon, earlier. Was it any good?"

"You're drunk. What do you expect?"

"I thought it would be my best sermon. Had a good one thought up, about the evils of looking for signs. Guess I read too much into Moctezuma. Didn't want to get garroted by the likes of you." He took a sip from the glass and rolled the liquor around his mouth like he was tasting a fine communal wine. Satisfied, he downed the rest of the glass. "Michael will do well here. He deserves a good position. Guess I set him up well. There'll be an ass in every damn seat next Sunday."

"I think we can afford a decent severance package for you."

"Fuck you, and fuck your severance package, Elliot."

"Well, excuse me!" the Elder yelled. "Just because you lost your faith doesn't mean you've got the right to get up in front of the congregation and behave like that."

"That's the difference between us," Ward said, inhaling deeply of his cigarette before he crushed it out on the expensive wood of the desk. "I've never once in my life, not even for a moment, doubted the existence of our God in Heaven. Never once."

"Could have fooled me. You're acting like a damned heathen."

"I'm acting like a person. That's all I am, Elliot. I'm a sinner, and I'm fucking tired of acting like I'm not."

"Well, you're doing a good job."

"Thank you."

"So, you've not lost your faith, and you're not a saint. Why'd you throw this all away? Is it because of your grandson?"

Ward turned in his seat, put both hands palms down on the surface of the desk, and looked Jones in the eye. "Don't talk about him."

"That's it, isn't it?"

"It's a beautiful world, Elliot. Maybe one day you'll remember that."

"I'm sorry the little boy drowned. There was nothing anyone could do."

"Don't you think I know that?" Ward said.

"Then what, Tommy? What?"

"You'll make sure all the paperwork is transferred, right?"

"Of course."

"I'm sure Michael will do great. May never give a sermon quite as good as the one I was forced to abandon today, but he'll do all right."

"Of course."

"And you, Elliot. I may not be able to do anything formally about your little situation, but I'm washing my hands of you."

"I'm working on that, Tommy."

"I know you think I'm doing this church a disservice, and I'm fine with that. But you, Elliot, you're the one destroying this place. You're the cancer. You're the leviathan lurking, the Devil in human form."

"Fuck you, Ward."

"I never really believed in the Devil until I met you. You yourself made me more secure in my faith. I hate that I have to thank you for that."

"Fuck you."

"I hear tell you have anything more to do with the Youth ministries, you'll have to answer to me."

"Fuck you, you heathen son of a bitch. Get out of this church."

"I'll send for my things," Ward said with a soft smile and stood up. He rolled down his sleeves, took his coat from the rack and put it on, picked up the bottle from the desk, and went to the office door.

"Oh," he said, pausing at the open door, the rest of Elders there, watching the two with morbid curiosity, "you know, there really isn't any consensus about old Moctezuma, really, about if that fellow really thought Cortez was a god. I doubt he did, but maybe he just saw how the tides were going to turn, and got caught up in the rapids."

NIRVANA

Hank was leaning his forehead against the window, and had been for the last two hours as he kept on pretending to sleep, like in the poem, that one little poem which put him on the bus, sitting with his head on the window, trying to get the drum circle in his head to stop pounding. The window was frosted over, and had been since he climbed aboard the night before. The bus had bad axles, and each bump was amplified sharply, and a well timed bump coupled with sudden turn managed to knock his head into the glass, seemingly at the epicenter of the headache. Hank groaned and cursed the window. The old man sitting beside him, with a long face and wrinkles that were all but indistinguishable from his acne scars, laughed. "Hangover?"

Hank nodded.

"You know what the absolute perfect cure for a hangover is, don't you, boy?"

"What's that?"

The old man reached into his coat pocket and pulled out a half-empty bottle of bourbon. "Hair of the dog, friend."

Any other day, Hank would have turned down the offer immediately, but considering it was four on a Friday morning and he was riding on a bus through the hills of North Carolina with snow coming down, he didn't hesitate to take the offered drink. There was a healthy burn down his throat but it didn't do anything for his head. The old man downed the rest of the bottle and started whistling an old blues melody. Hank leaned against the window.

The old man got off in a town Hank had never heard of and in his stead a woman with two small children got on. They did nothing for his head.

He concentrated on the sound of the engine, the tires on the road, and the voices of the other riders. It seemed to him a pleasant sort of white noise that he willingly fell in to, until the grinding of the breaks and the sudden stop sent his head forward into the seat in front of him.

It was still dark and snowing. The bus was parked outside a cafe and the passengers were filing out into the cold. Hank joined them inside.

Inside, he sat at the counter and ordered a cup of coffee from the young waitress with a thrill. Country music played softly over hidden speakers. The waitress, whose nametag said Pamela, had curly, dirty blond hair and green eyes. She brought his coffee black and asked if he'd like anything else.

"Just coffee for now, please." She nodded and went off to help some of the other passengers. The coffee was particularly good. He drank it in slow, steady sips, concentrating on the moment. It was good.

"Want a refill?" Pamela asked when the other passengers were content with their food.

"Sure."

"What's your name?"

"Chinaski. Hank Chinaski." A lie.

"So where are you headed, Hank Chinaski?" she asked as she filled his cup.

"Right here, I'm thinking."

"Really?"

"Really.

"Why's that?"

"Because of a poem." Concerning the odd look she gave him, he continued, "This poem, it's about a kid on a bus, riding through the hills of North Carolina. Bus stops at a café and the kid drinks his coffee and eats some food and never wants to leave the café."

"Sounds like quite a poem."

"It is."

"So, you're reenacting it."

"I guess. Trying to find out what it was like for the poet. Or the protagonist or whatever. The poem always had this beauty to it. Guess I wanted to see it myself."

The bus driver, a big guy named Burt, called out, "Anyone heading to Boone, the bus will be leaving in five minutes."

"Well, better drink up if you're going to make the bus," Pamela said.

"The kid in the poem, he got back on that bus. I'm thinking of seeing what it'd be like not to."

"Stuck in a backwoods town with no ride. About like that, I'd imagine."

"Perhaps, but what else do I have to do?"

"You could try working."

"Yeah, got to be in tomorrow morning."

"Quite the wild one, aren't you?"

"Hardly."

The other passengers, they began to get up, filing past and paying Pamela in cash. Hank watched them go out to the snow and get back on the bus. After a few minutes, it started rolling. Pamela watched him sitting there, watching the bus leave him behind.

"How's it feel?"

"Beautiful."

And he sat there, drinking his coffee. Sometime later he ordered a ham sandwich, and after that, he enjoyed a slice of apple pie. He drank some more coffee, and it was good, and for that he was particularly glad.

The sun came up as it was supposed to.

INCARNATION

He chased the ocean, the needle pegged as he roared down from the hills, a puddle growing in the boot pressed hard against the floorboard, his lungs burning to scare the dark away. For several long minutes he held his breath, wishing the stars a longer domain, the moon threatening with each slowing beat its descent. He trailed tobacco smoke in his wake and cursed each moment that death didn't creep into the cold passenger seat. The radio danced with static interspersed with a station broadcasting communiqués for those hanging cold in their continual war. From his stomach a trickle of blood leaked downward. Sparks and fireflies danced in his vision as he struggled to keep the tires between the yellow. From one horizon to the other was nothing but black, like the space between stars, the nothingness of the heavens, the eyes that haunt him in the daytime. The engine angrily growled as the interstate evened and took to a straightaway, the foothills nothing but a memory, the mountain a leviathan hidden in the night's abyss.

Three quarts of blood, a hundred miles, and several hours back, the night began with a young woman reading a thick book in an empty bar. A sliver of Norteño hung in the air, the bajo sexto carrying the melody of a woman trying to kill her husband after one strike too many. Cornelio the barman kept his distance, stepping forward only when she raised an empty glass. When Cornelio first served the woman she'd had been a girl of sixteen, as striking as the woman who sat before him now. A Criollo twice her age had put his hand on her thigh and when she spat to the dirt he laughed and called her 'Indio.' She shattered his nose with the bottle of tequila she was enjoying. As the man moaned on the floor, liquor and blood mixing with the dust his movements stirred, the girl pulled the knife strapped under her dress and removed his right ear with a slight motion. The Criollo never showed his crooked face again and Cornelio always kept enough añejo on hand. Over the next decade, the barman watched her mature, her coffee skin darken under the sun, her eyes grow hard and her blade-hand quicker. She raised her glass and Cornelio did his job in silence. She mumbled, 'Gracias,' and he smiled.

The white man, his pants covered with cement dust, slid silently into the bar and took a chair beside the woman, placing a tamale still wrapped in cornhusk on the bar. She marked her place in the book of poems with a pink rose petal and looked to Cornelio, saying with a soft voice, 'Uno más, por favor.' She turned to the man and grimaced. 'You are late, Güero.' Her English was thick with accent but clear. Her eyes danced over his features before finding their home observing nothing.

'How are you, Yncarnación?' Güero took a sip of the drink Cornelio set down before him and smiled. 'Delicious, gracias.'

'You are late.' She lit a cigarillo, letting the velvet smoke play around her tongue before finishing her drink.

'Long drive, short notice. You have a job for me?' He unwrapped the tamale and took a bite. Green peppers were buried under the corn.

'I did not request you for your company.'

He said, swallowing before speaking, 'I know, hermosa. What can I do for you?'

'I want you to visit the King of Cups and the Page of Wands.'

'You want them dead?'

'I want you to deliver to each man a letter.'

* * *

Each moment blowing past like the obscured landscape required more effort to keep the accelerator to the floor, his eyes open. The car was a bullet and the momentum was aimed at the coast, cutting through the night as it roared closer to the target. Shock had set in and the chasm in his gut was rimmed with ice. His hand shook on the wheel as he weaved between cavernous potholes. The government had never seen the need to install streetlights this far out, nor would any policía risk themselves in land as hostile.

He started hacking and had brought his hand up in an unconscious effort to catch the expulsion and the front left wheel came an inch within digging downward into the road. A flash of the tire popping and the car swerving hard to the right, the weight in the rear moving ahead, the kinetic force pushing the frame over as the sound of metal grinding flooded through his ears, the ceiling below crashing in, his face slamming first against the steering wheel then shattering the side window, killing him before anything else had the chance. He pulled hard and slung gravel, half the car dipping into the ditch before he could right his path. His pulse vibrated in every inch of his body and the dribble under his shirt amplified to a gush as his vision faded until he brought the palm of his left hand sharply against his cheek. He pushed a breath through his nostrils and laughed until he fell back into a cough.

Pimotl stood outside the church building watching the ocean beat against the shore, the moon slowly sliding downward, out of the sky. Towards the east the horizon was a dark red. His milk-colored eyes took in everything, as he did each morning, and he let out a sigh that carried the previous day's sins out on the breeze. Pimotl's was a ritual borrowed from the man's father, long since resigned to the dust. Each day could be your last, the old man had said, and I don't want to walk into heaven without seeing the sunrise again. Pimotl's father had founded La Iglesia de Juan de la

Cruz in early days of the last century, and even after the congregation stopped coming, the old man had continued the daily pilgrimage, and Pimotl in turn. His men, soldiers and bodyguards, questioned why he would always go there alone, given how easy it would be for a bullet to find its way there, how they would gladly walk the shore and give him company. Pimotl's eyes would turn to stone and for several weeks, until hostilities broke out again, no man would say a thing to him as he left before the moon died and was he reborn in the sun. From a great distance he could hear the car driving towards him, the engine roaring and the tires slinging rock. For a moment, the thought that this would be the last day played out in his mind. Pimotl smiled and remained at his vigil.

Güero left Yncarnación with two letters, each piece of paper sealed with candle wax. The first was for a man named Adolfo, who Yncarnación had called the Page of Wands. The closer of the two deliveries. Güero drove across the small town, the sun slowly fading into the dust that hung like a fog. His pistol sat on the passenger seat. A wrinkled man stood hunched on a corner holding a rifle. A priest laughed with a young whore over a bottle of cerveza outside of another bar, where narcocorridos played and the thugs drank without fear. Every eye turned to the Güero as he passed, then forgot about him when his taillights disappeared. Adolfo was the patrón of a hacienda past the outskirts, where coyotes and crows scored the night. Güero pulled up the stone road through the open gate. Three gauchos stood smoking cornhusk cigarettes around a slaughtered pig, its insides steaming in the dirt. They watched as Güero parked and left his car, the pistol tucked into his belt. He called out to them, asking where he could find Adolfo. One spat and pointed to the great house that stood like a pearl at the beginning of a great desert. Güero had taken three of the six stairs to the main door when it swung open, exposing Adolfo to the world. He was light skinned, his face crooked with deep scars mapped out from the nose.

'Did Yncarnación send you?' A hand rose unconsciously to where his right ear used to be.

Güero stepped up, even with Adolfo, and reached into his coat and brought forth the letter. 'She sent me to deliver this to you.'

Adolfo glanced down at the exposed gun in Güero's belt before staring at the paper offered. His fat fingers took the letter and ripped it open, the wax crumbling to the stone the two men stood on. His nostrils flared as he read and he looked to Güero, asking if this was a joke.

'I'm just a messenger here. Couldn't begin to tell you what she wrote.' Güero shifted his weight from one foot to the other, not able to find comfort.

'She sends you, a pistolero, to deliver this piece of bullshit?' The paper crumbled in Adolfo's fist.

'That does appear to be the case.' Güero had the overwhelming desire to hold his gun.

'And you have no idea what it is she wrote?'

'No, I don't. She wanted me to deliver a letter to you and to an old man.'

'Pimotl?'

'Yes.'

Adolfo looked down, spreading the letter out and looking over its contents again, his lips moving as he read, before dropping it. Both men watched its descent. When it hit the stone, Adolfo spat and reached behind his back, bringing a blade flashing out into the night and burying it deep in Güero's stomach. The wounded man took a staggered step backward, the knife sliding out and Adolfo stepping forward to deliver another blow. Güero's left hand covered the hole as his right found the pistol's grip and he hefted it forward. The muzzle rested for a moment on Adolfo's forehead as Güero's index finger searched for the trigger. The hammer fell on the chambered bullet, and it passed through Adolfo's head and shattered the plate-glass window on the dead man's front door.

When Adolfo hit the ground, the gauchos yelled, the sound muffled by the wail in Güero's ears as he moved the gun and stopped them in the dust. A woman came from the inside of the house, her knees grinding on shattered glass as she fell over the man and choked on her curses. Güero kept the gun on the three men as he left a trail of blood down the stairs and made his way back to his car. Flies found their way to the dead pig and each man glared thick with hate, but not one stepped forward. Güero fell into the driver's seat and slammed the door. The tires spun before the car found traction and Güero was gone.

He fell out of the car and at Pimotl's feet, his hand shaking as he lifted the letter up like a prayer. The old man looked down with a smile and helped him up to his feet, supporting the white man's weight as they walked towards the shore. The two men sat on the cold sand and watched as the sun grew, a sliver of bright light at the horizon of a dead night. Güero's fingers clutched the paper, refusing to do anything but deliver his charge. Pimotl removed his arm from the dying man's shoulder and received the letter. He carefully broke the seal and spread the paper over his knees, ignoring the spots of red. Güero did not take his eyes from the ocean. They sat for several long minutes with the sound of the waves crashing, birds calling from the distance.

When Pimotl asked if he would like to see the letter, Güero softly shook his head, saying it did not concern him. The old man smiled and together they watched the sun rise. The sun became too bright and Güero closed his eyes, his head nodding forward, his hand still on the wound. It leaked no more and Pimotl rose, leaving the young man in the sand. Pimotl walked past the church and lit a cigarillo. Güero's door swung on the hinge. Pimotl drove in search of his daughter.

Güero sat on the beach, the spray of the waves washing over his face, until the tide came in, and even still.

LEVIATHAN

My father talked about them when I was a kid, when I sat around the fire and listened to those older than me talk and laugh, the bottles in their hands getting emptier and lighter, as the night dragged on like an anchor. My father liked to talk about those monsters, those behemoths that came from nowhere, juggernauts that raged at whoever was foolish enough to be in their path. Worse than the leviathans from the Bible, from myths, they could attack in even calm weather, with the sea smooth as glass, a reflection of the perfect sky, nothing save the sun in the top half of the orb. Towards the end of the evening, he would have so much drink inside him, he would actually tell us, me, the story he refused to divulge when sober. He followed his father out to the sea, as I would him. My father was on a boat captained by an elder named Long, who some said was as old as the sea. He had been with those who founded our village when my great-grandfather was a boy. When the water was calm and their nets were out, Long talked about the dangers of the sea, the almost evil nature of an uncaring expanse. "I've seen many die out here," Long said. "I've seen the best examples of men taken as quickly as a blink, bodies consumed by the abyss as if it were nothing. I've seen the sea itself rain down death." Long said, "this water will kill you if it wants, make no mistake about that." The old man lit a cigarette rolled in a corn husk, and as he struck his match, it was blown out by a swift shift of the wind. My father said his stomach lurched as the boat dropped with the lowering of the sea. The world went dark, as they were in a valley of water, and a mountain loomed above, and an avalanche came descending like the fury of God. The wave came crashing like the heavens on the final day, and the boat buried under the rolling mass. My father fought, and tried to find his way to the surface, but under that force he was not sure which was up, which down. For a time, he thought he was dead, and the struggle, the pressure of a world of water above him was what it must feel for a soul leaving the body. He stopped the fight, thinking it only right to accept God's will, and then there was an explosion of air, and the world was right, the sky above and the water around him. The wave was towards the horizon, fleeing the wreckage it had made. The boat was capsized, but in one piece. He managed to get it right, being a small vessel, and he climbed aboard. He waited for Long, but the man never surfaced. He waited for hours, days, under the apathetic sun, the callous moon, and then there was a spot on the horizon, and for a moment he thought Death was coming for him, having missed its first effort. My father was rescued by the men of his village. As they brought him aboard their boat, no one asked where Long was; as they gave him bread and fresh water, not a word was said. When my father saw me to the dock for my first trip to sea, he told me, unaware he had in the past, of that wave, of the uncaring gods of the sea. I thought of them, of his words, as the blue expanse dropped abruptly, as the daylight was obscured, as that great titan descended upon the boat many years after I heard the story, and the currents ripped me from safety, as my lungs filled with brine, as the dark took me for its own, I thought of those words, and how I would not pass them to my young.

THE GREAT
SCHISM

John the Baptist, his head alone on the silver, was the first to go, shattering like so many hearts. First time didn't take, but he was prepared, and tore another scrap from his soiled undershirt, stuffed it into the bottle's lip like a gag, lit the scrap with his daddies' brass Zippo, the one with "Fuck Communism" engraved across it like John Wayne's; he wheeled back and threw the bottle through Noah's ark and the it broke on a pew and there were no stopping things.

They found him sitting in the middle of the cracked parking lot when the fire trucks got there, first the VFD then the county crew, him sitting there under an oak they said as old as the church, as the country itself, smoking his way through a pack and drinking through the rest of his bottles, the gas can empty beside him.

You see what happened, boy, the captain asked as his crew got to work, running hose and already sweating through their shirts. It had spread at that point to the newer additions to the church, long since done it's damage to the centuries-old building, and there was no hope of saving anything but the foundations.

Went up fast. Once it got spread over the pews, the floor, all the windows crashed in on themselves, likely to get more fuel for the beast.

The captain nodded, watched his men as they worked in vain for a minute, then walked his way over to the unmarked cruiser that came to watch like it all was a matinee. A window rolled down as he approached.

Hi, Mike.

Llew. What's the cause, he asked before taking a drink of his fresh coffee. Had been a slow night.

Arson, by the looks.

How you figure that?

Boy over there did it, I'd wager.

Lovely.

Boy didn't seem in a rush to leave, so the detective let him finish his smoke, him his own coffee, before getting out of the car and walking a slow, calculated pace over to the gnarled old tree, one the kids of the area called the old man on account of some knots that resembled it's namesake. Mike took the time crossing the uneven pavement sizing the boy up, noting the muddy jeans, torn and dirty shirt that may have been white at some point but was reduced to a piss yellow in the light of the fire. He was far enough to be out of the heat, but Mike saw the withered leaves on the tree and figured it had been worse earlier. The summer night was still hot, the air thick with smoke and water, and would get no more comfortable once the haze cleared. He felt his shirt get sticky on the way over, like the feeling of his bedsheets the night prior, after he and his wife had their fill.

Hidy, he said for effect.

Hi. Boy was watching the crew at their work, already winning but the inch to victory nigh late.

You're Martin Boyd's kid, aren't you? His youngest?

Yessir.

Junior, ain't you? The smell on the boy was unmistakable.

Some call me, yessir. Hand was shaking as he took a drag.

See it go down?

Yessir, I did. His teeth were chattering like a blizzard was coming down.

See Marty taught you well. Manners, I mean.

Yessir, he did.

What'd you see?

It all.

See who did it?

After a shallow grave breath, said, Couldn't really see myself.

Come on.

Yessir.

Mike put him in a room at the station with a can of Coke and told the boy he'd be back in a spell, then went out and over to his desk, most of the other's gone for the night save them who didn't see as their work was done, or those who hadn't anyone to go home too. He checked the boy's name into the computer. Was just past a minor so there wasn't anything more than sworn affidavit from five years back. Goddammit, he said like a prayer. His superior came out of the bathroom whipping his hands on his pants, went over to Mike's desk and leaned against it.

Leland.

Open and shut, right.

Yes, sir.

Don't like it.

No, sir.

He got a file?

No, just a victim's statement.

The Brown case?

Yes, sir.

Goddammit. Mike couldn't help but grin a bit. Leland saw and followed suit for a moment, his nicotine yellow teeth like a child's first, small and set apart. Is there a retraction?

Yes, sir.

That wasn't a good time, here, you know. Not for Brown, least, the poor bastard. Deacon over there for some such a decade, then all that shit comes piling up. Recollect even Reverend Ward tried to speak for him, old friends as they were, but he weren't a very good character witness at the time. The shit you find on a computer, even with that Brown didn't deserve what this town did to him.

Every statement was withdrawn after they found him roped up, weren't they?

Most of all, yep. There was talk some of them were meant

for someone else there, but the town buried it after Brown went and did what he did.

Was too much, I guess.

I reckon.

Detective Mike Todd walked in with a pen, pencil, and a paper cup of coffee for himself. You tired?

No, sir.

We could put you in a cell, let you get some rest, do this all in the morning.

No, sir. Let's just get it on over with.

Right. The first sip was bitter, the second a weed that grew on him. He put the pencil on the paper and pushed it across the table, over graffiti from others that had sat where the boy sat. Just need a confession, here, but first, well, why'd you do it?

Went to that church my whole life.

Me too. Baptized there in sixty-eight.

Few years before my time. They partook in a small laugh, the boy's like the wind passing through a scarecrow.

Find my name in your computers?

Yeah.

In relation to Deacon Brown.

Yeah.

Told my folks, after a couple years, what had happened to me. Was about the time that stuff was found on his computer at the church. Didn't say who, scared, I guess, ashamed, whatever, they put two and two together.

Came out to five.

Yeah. Guess everyone else's math was wrong, too. Always liked Deacon Brown.

Me, too.

He was off, everyone seen that, but he never as much as touched my shoulder in passing. After, folks left, more than when the Reverend did what he did.

So, why tonight?

Always liked the church. Until what happened happened. Then it was just a building. God wasn't there.

No, he wasn't. He's else, they say.

They say. Can't burn him down. Fire took everything else, crosses and hymnals and communion wine, but not him. He picked up the pencil and wrote out a sentence, wrote his name out, then above that signed it.

Can't burn him down.

HALFWAY CROOKS

"You'll have a hell of a lot of time to think when you drive home," Doyle said from the passenger seat. "You'll go through a long stretch out in the hills without the radio. Only thing you'll hear is the coyotes calling to each other. You'll have nothing but time and I'm betting you'll be doing some thinking. Use it well, and remember why it is you'll be doing what it is you're going to do, why you've got that gun on you."

Doyle coughed harshly, doubling over and burying his flush, ravaged face in his handkerchief, his elbows crushing the hat that was perched on his knee, before he rolled down the window and spat into the outer dark. He sat back and dabbed at the trickle of red that hung at the corner of his mouth, at the scar that expanded his smile unnaturally.

Nearly thirty years back, though he'd never told me the story, someone put a blade into his mouth and, first, slit to the right almost to his cauliflowered ear, then to the left. I'd seen a picture of the days after that, after the stitches went in: my dad standing beside him, the two wearing expensive suits, Doyle with a revolver in his right hand, slung over my father's shoulders. Doyle had the look of a rabid hyena, his face torn, his eyes those of a man looking to do some killing.

The eyes in the seat beside me were of a man looking to die. Spilling blood, necessary or not, was never something I took easily to.

"You okay?" I asked. Hands steady on the wheel, moving slow through the snow coming at the car like a meteor shower. Doyle took a pull from his flask before pressing his moist temple against the passenger-side window.

"I'll survive," he said, turning his lips and flashing that cadaverous smile of his.

"How much farther is it?" I lit a cigarette and glanced at Doyle, slumped against the door. When I exhaled, the smoke lingered, floating between us like a ghost before catching the wind and sliding out into the night.

"Another ten miles or so. We'll crest a hill and when we start to fall, the road will split a dead tobacco field in two." He reached out for the smoke and I passed the cigarette over to him. He inhaled and I had to hide my revulsion. Doyle moved to hand the smoke back. I shook my head, letting him keep it before repeating the one-handed ritual.

"How long's it been since you've been here?"

"Christ, I don't know. Ten years? Twenty? Doesn't matter, it'll be there, right where I told you."

"Time goes by, maybe the land changed?"

"The world don't change near as much as you'd think. Give it a couple decades and you'll see."

"Like you're a damned philosopher or something. Look at where we're from. Hopewell ain't near the town it was when I was growing up."

"New buildings, sure, but the people ain't ever changed. Drunks and preachers and folk going about their lives. Maybe a bit more users than when I was your age, but when we were passing through town on the way out, I saw more home than not."

Four hours back, as the sun was making its fall behind the thick, iron-colored clouds, I went cruising through town, stopping by his house down off of Mt. Holly. He wasn't home and his dog-- an ugly mutt, part bulldog and seemingly part wolf-- wouldn't stop growling and snapping at me through the chain-link fence.

Doyle wasn't there so I cut down Beatties Ford and hit McCoy, taking that past a lone llama standing sentinel in a barren field. Every other field in the area was filled with cows or horses, goats or chickens, but that one always had a single llama looking out as the cars drove on by. A small house, closer to a shack, stood alone in a clearing. The lawn was empty of anything signifying life. Were it not for the bicycle perched by the door or the smoke flowing from the chimney, one'd think it was abandoned.

I couldn't help a smile remembering Frank, the man who lived there. When Puckett's Gas Station was open, he used to walk up there every day for a coke and a biscuit. Puckett's had turned into a barbecue joint a few years back.

From McCoy, I took Kerns a mile and pulled into Frayer's.

"Think you could pull over?" Doyle asked as the car moved along a curve along the hills that were quickly turning to mountain. To the right was a vista of lights shining in the distance like stars reflecting off the surface of a calm lake.

"Got to piss?" I looked back to the road as the village below was obscured by trees.

"Something fierce." His voice had grown thinner and could barely be heard over the wind that blew away our cigarette smoke.

"You're getting old."

Doyle grunted and started to shimmy in his seat. "Don't I know it. Can't even drink properly no more. Been getting up damn near every hour at night to use the bathroom." His legs were shaking up and down with the strain.

"I doubt there's anywhere for you to do your thing." The car started to dance in the wind as he hummed an old jazz number.

"Hell, as dead as this road is, just pull over near a bush and I'll do what needs to be done."

"Fine by me. Just not in the car." Past the long curve, the road straightened out and I slowed the car and parked it on the side. It was bitter cold and the clouds threatened ever more snow. The moon held no station up in the sky.

I turned off the headlights and the road was overtaken by shadows save a spot down near the end where a streetlight stood faint like a candle at the end of a long tunnel. We opened our doors simultaneously as I pulled the keys from the ignition. We'd been in the car for so long our bodies were on their way to atrophy. When Doyle finally stood fully erect, his knees and back creaked like the sound of a gun in the distance. I strode to the back and leaned against the trunk as he took a few light steps over the ditch and stood at the brush with his back to me.

Pulling my lighter from my pocket, I bounced it a couple times up and down before removing the pack and jostled a smoke out and between my lips. He whistled and sighed as he relieved himself, and I flipped the top of the lighter back, striking the flint and putting the flame to the tip. The cherry took to life quickly and I stood there, watching him and absorbing the fading warmth of the lighter's silver casing. Etched on the front were my father's initials.

They'd let me stay in the room with him at the hospital while they waited on the funeral home to pick him up. He was stiff and wrong under the blanket and I sat there in the one chair, looking at him and asking myself why it was I didn't cry. When the guys got there with the gurney, I went down to the bathroom.

Between the men's and the women's, I drank from the water fountain until I had to catch my breath, the water cool and clean and absolutely perfect and there was no one around, no patients or visitors or nurses and they came, tardy tears, even though for many long years I'd hated my old man, taken his fists and between the two of us every foul word in the language was used, I stood there for many long minutes with wet cheeks and when I went back, the old man was gone.

I asked a nurse at the front desk for a box and gathered up all his personal items. Sitting at the bottom of a drawer in the bedside table was that lighter. I slid it into my pocket and not a day went by that I didn't keep it there.

When Doyle was finished, he turned to me with his stretched smile and told me, "You know, I bought that lighter for your dad when he got back from Korea. Figured the man ought to have something good for himself after what it was he went through. Later that day, he met me at

Frayer's and handed me this.' He pulled out his flask and twisted off the top. He handed it to me but I declined. 'He said he never did want to be in debt to anyone. Course, that was bullshit. We're always in debt to someone in this world. I took it and thanked him."

"Can't imagine him giving anything to anyone," I said, moving back to the driver's seat. Doyle followed suit, sinking back into the seat.

"Lord, I needed that. You gave your dad too much trouble over the years, and I understand that, but the man did everything he could for you. Hell, when your mother left, I'd slide him some of my own gigs so he could have a bit more money for you."

I turned the ignition and the car started up with a rough idle because of the cold, but when I put some pressure on the gas and shifted into drive, it fell into place. "I don't doubt that at all, Doyle. Just wish the two of us would've had some of the better days."

"Don't we all, boy?" As we moved closer to the streetlight, Doyle asked "Want to see a magic trick?"

I shrugged- "Sure."

He cocked his right hand like a pistol, forefinger for the barrel and thumb for the hammer. He aimed straight at the lamp and getting closer, he said, dryly, "Bang," like a kid shooting a robber. The light went out and we passed through the opaque night.

There were only two cars outside of Frayer's. One belonged to Sam Hall, the bartender, and the other was Doyle's, a white Lincoln Town Car the size of a tank. The tires gleamed like obsidian under the fading daylight. I parked beside his ride and went inside, forcing myself to take each step. Sure enough, Hall had a bottle of bourbon sitting between them. Each man held a tumbler, and they were laughing about a joke they'd told each other thousands of times over the years. Hall, a former boxer from the eastern half of the state, went ashen when he saw me. Doyle looked to see who walked in and smiled when we made eye contact. His thin, gray hair was greasy and sticking up at every angle. "Right on time, boy."

"You ready?" I asked.

"Does it have to be tonight?" Hall said. He poured a couple fingers into his glass and emptied it immediately.

"The boy has a job to do," Doyle said, motioning for another glass, "and I ain't going to be the one to stop him. Want a drink?"

"Not tonight," I said, though I was thirsty as a soul in Hell.

"If you're sure," Doyle said before taking a long drink.

"Hate to see you go," Hall said. He reached forward a fat hand and patted Doyle on the shoulder, making a packing sound that echoed through the empty bar.

"You'll be fine, you old ass. Put this on my tab," Doyle said as he stood up and took his gray fedora from the bar and placed it crookedly on his head.

"You know it," Hall said as Doyle moved past me to the door. I took a last look at Hall, his eyes red from the dusty room.

Outside, the sky was a bright red close to the horizon and darker, more claret above. We stood before our cars and I asked which car he'd prefer to take.

"We'll take yours long as I can smoke."

"Course you can."

He pulled his keys from his suit pocket and handed them to me.

It was exactly as Doyle had described it. The road moved over a steep hill, and when the car hit the apex, the view opened up to a large, dead field bisected by the asphalt. At the base of the rise, on the western side, was a small cemetery lined with a stone wall. "Here we are," Doyle said, his voice gaining strength the closer we got. His eyes were effulgent and that smile was wider than even his lips seemed capable of. "Park there, at the front."

When we reached the bottom, I acquiesced and parked on the opposite side of the road from the graveyard's large, wrought iron gate. When I turned the car off, we sat there for several moments, the two of us taking in the view. The wall looked to have been built around the time of the Civil War, and what few stones I could make out inside held the same classic aesthetic.

"How'd you find this place?" I said.

Doyle let out a sigh. "I brought my wife up here one year for a date, before we got married. We had a whole picnic basket set up, and I had blankets and wine. I told her we were going to have a grand old time, find some quiet place to pull over. It was a nice day, really. Later that year, we came up again, just before we got married. It was winter and when we pulled up over that hill, this whole little valley was covered in the softest snow you'd ever seen. We pulled over and walked between the rows and when we came to the back of the cemetery, we saw this, I don't know what you want to call it, a blight out in all that perfect white. We jumped over the wall and walked out to it, our feet sinking down to the ankles, and when we got there we saw it was a cross, a ten-foot-tall wooden cross burned to a crisp laying there where it'd fell. It was still steaming. I ain't been back here since."

"And you picked this place?"

"I picked this place because no matter the ugliness we saw that day, it'd always be beautiful to me. Makes me think of her, God rest her soul. Couldn't think of a better place, really."

I nodded, there not being anything else for me to say. We got out of the car, him moving faster than his years, me the old man, regretting the trip, what was about to come. He walked up to the gate and put his face between the bars like a kid looking at the full Christmas spread. "It ain't changed a bit," he said before turning to me with a simple smile faded for a beat when he remembered why we were here. "I should have brought you up here when you were a kid. When your dad did his bid, when you were living with Lucy and me."

"Bet I'd have loved it."

"I know you would have. Come on, not in here," he said, moving along the outer perimeter of the wall to the back of the field. We walked further out into the field, the small coating of fresh snow crunching beneath our shoes, until he stopped and turned to face me. We stood a pace apart and he nodded. When I hesitated, didn't do the job, he chuckled. "It's all right, boy. Really, it is."

He reached into his coat and brought forth his flask. A gift from my father. He unscrewed the top, took a long pull while cocking his head back and gasping when he came up for air. He offered me a drink and I nodded, stepping forward. Our fingers touched as he handed it to me. I repeated his motions, savoring the burn that killed the world for only a moment. When I tried to pass it back, he held a hand up. "You keep it. Seems fitting."

"You sure about this?" A flock of birds a ways off from us gave us no mind as they went about their lives, trying to breech the blinding white, the frozen snow.

"What, like you'd let me just walk away?"

"I would. You know I would, too. I'd go back and tell Ralph-" my voice broke and my jaw shook until I managed to catch myself. "I'd tell Ralph that I did the deed and he'd nod and forget about it."

"But you're a man of your word, and I hate that I've got to ask this, boy, but I'd rather it be you." My eyes went bleary as I pushed my hand into my coat. He reached up a hand and adjusted his fedora, straightened his tie, made sure his shirt was tucked in.

"Are you ready?"

He stood unimaginably tall and proud there before me. "I am. There ain't no halfway crooks in this life, and I've got to own up to what it is I did." I removed my hand and held it down by my leg, my fingers taping rapidly, without rhythm.

"I know."

"And you had best take care of my dog."

"I will."

"Love you, boy."

"Love you, Uncle Doyle."

He smiled, and for a moment I did too. I lifted and held my hand forward and when the hammer fell, the birds gathered in the field took flight to escape the furious noise and the crushing silence that remained as he dropped. Those birds flew as high as they could out into the night.

GOD USE ME AS A HAMMER

It was the sensation of warmth at his toes that jarred Tommy. He drifted upwards from the haze, his eyes creaked open, breaking the crust of sleep. A sharp pinch ran through his ankles when he tried to find comfort, a similar pain in his wrists. He followed a tunnel towards clarity and found his bedside lamp to be a pale star burning in the heavens. He was bound. There was a spark at the foot of his bed and a shadow looming above. He tried to speak a cursory word but his throat prickled with sand. The warmth grew in his lower extremities and congealed into a white-hot searing. His nose caught the scent of cooking meat.

A grunt like a cornered beast escaped his lips and the shadow looked up, its eyes glowing in the

low light. It moved away from Tommy's feet and took the form of a man. Bristles of fever sweat bloomed on Tommy's forehead as he observed the long, black coat over the plain suit, the hat perched like a gargoyle, the welder's torch in the right hand, and then the sharp eyes. The man turned the blade down low and set it on the table, neither man breaking the gaze. His body hummed from the blisters forming over his heel.

The hand disappeared into the recesses of a pocket and brought forth a small square. It shook loose a cigarette into its waiting twin where it was lifted aloft to the man's lips and lit by the torch into a firefly calling out to its kin. Two fingers brought the butt down to Tommy's lips. He breathed in and the vibrations wracking through his body slowed. The hand reached back and offered a small, crumpled picture. The man held it above Tommy's face and finally broke its silence: "Look."

Tommy acquiesced, and in the bare light made out the form of a girl, the hair framing her plain

face curled and frayed. Eyes bright with a strength of joy Tommy had never known, her smile a movement at the edge of his memories. He knew her face, and why the man was there.

"I know you are not a nice person," the man said, moving the picture back to the safety of his

pocket, "and I know you recognize her." The man took the cigarette from Tommy's lips and inhaled its smoke. "I even know the odds of me finding her, alive and unharmed, are rather low. The thing is," he paused, turning the smoke around in his fingers, "that you are going to tell me exactly where she is and what you did to her." He tapped the butt until the ash fell to the ground like dirty snow and once the cherry was clear, he slowly moved it until it was an inch from Thomas's eye. "This is the only moment of grace you will receive."

Thomas was silent for several heartbeats, and then he spoke.

PRIEST
AND
PISTOL

When the killers gave Eduard the choice between the machete and the tire, it was sometime after midnight. They had been beating him since nightfall.

They broke down the front door and flooded into his home. Seven men, most in gaudy, expensive clothes, brandishing pistols and shotguns and blades coated in tissue and dry blood. Their leader was dressed as a priest but had no collar around his throat. They struck Eduard and put a gun to his face, a knife to his throat. The Priest asked if Eduard would like to go for a drive as his men tore up the house. They put a bag over his head and drove in circles as the sun descended from the sky. They cursed and threatened to be there for his wife when she came home. The Priest silenced them with a bullet. Eduard could feel the white heat of it pass close to his face, smell the spray of powder burning through the cloth over his face. A weight slumped against him and the rest of the ride was quiet. The wind cut through the broken window and Eduard could smell the desert.

The killers took bets behind the circle of headlights. The blade was the most popular option, but Eduard read the newspapers and he knew it would not be as quick or simple as a beheading. They would start with his feet, chopping them off at the ankles and tying a tourniquet around the stumps. He would sit in his pain for maybe an hour, getting to know it as something real. He would scream and try to crawl to safety but they would be there to kick him back into the arena of cars. Then they would take his knees. The killers made a game out of it, trying to draw out the murder for as long as possible.

Choose the tire, the Priest said, bent above the prone form of Eduard. It will hurt; there is nothing I can do about that, but it will be over with sooner than you would think. The smoke will put you to sleep and it'll be done.

The stars were out, and this far from the world they saw everything. Every finger had been broken, some several times. Eduard's teeth were smashed from his jaw, his blood trailing down his face, his throat. Eduard asked for the tire and the killers groaned. A voice said, We can still use the machete, but the Priest cut him down.

There is no joy in this for me. I am a soldier.

Eduard wanted to ask why, but he found no words. It did not matter, though. This was the death he was born into. Two killers came and handcuffed each of his arms to a chain. The chains were attached to the bumper of a car. The men behind the wheels took just enough pressure off of the brake peddles to pull Eduard to his feet, his arms extended, shoulders and elbows and wrists out of sockets. The Priest stood before Eduard and placed a comforting hand on his chest.

I will say a prayer for you if you will do the same for me.

Two of the killers put a tire around Eduard's neck. His face and chest were splashed with the gasoline pooled inside. Each breath was fought for. One of the killers laughed. The Priest shot him in the center of his back and ordered him to be left for the coyotes. Eduard begged and the Priest relented. A match was lit and dropped into the tire. His screams echoed through the night and birds of prey mocked him. The Priest did not lie, it was over fast. As the flames spread, over his body and into his lungs, the Priest put a pistol to Eduard's forehead, but it was not needed. The man went quiet. They unhooked the chains and the body fell, flesh still smoldering into the dawn. The smoke and the ashes caught the wind and were carried across the desert, to the coast and over the ocean.

PADRE NUESTRO

Hadn't seen my old man for going on a decade when I got the call. My brother Thiago's muffled voice came over the line, the frequencies compressed but the force behind his words carried all I needed to know. He's dead, I said, and Thiago's silence was all the confirmation I needed. Happened the day before. The old man had keeled over in the liquor store, taking a shelf's worth of mescal with him. Thiago told me he'd been in some town over the border, had been there for the last few years. When I put the phone down, I went to my boss and told him I needed a few days off. He looked at me over his glasses, his feet propped up on a desk that cost more than a year's worth of rent for me, and said that'd be a problem. We've got a big deadline next week and need all hands on deck, he told me. I went back to my desk and then pretended to be sick. Went home and packed a week's worth of clothes, loaded up the gas tank, and was gone.

Took two days, through Iowa and Nebraska, Colorado and Utah, through the southern tip of Nevada to California, only stopping for gas and to piss into ditches off the side of desolate roads. I'd never seen the desert before. The world here was the memory of destruction, the end of us all come early. Thiago called as I passed by the Devil's Playground. He'd found a funeral home willing to cremate our father. I asked about his last wishes and Thiago said, All he wanted was to be spread somewhere beautiful. I told him how far out I was and we promised to meet up there.

Most of what I knew about Rodolfo, our father, I learned from Thiago. He was a giant of a man who supported his kin on the billiard tables. Even though he left before I was aware of it, he still sent my mother some cash every month until I turned twenty. I was in middle school when I met him for the first time. He'd been passing through Illinois and took Thiago and me to a fútbol game. He came to my high school graduation and that was the last time I saw my father.

I met Thiago in a small diner across the border from where it had happened. Last I saw of him was Christmas, where I'd spent a weekend with him and his family. We sat in silence, neither of us able to catch the right words. Rodolfo hadn't wanted his ashes in the church, hadn't wanted any memories spoken or tears shed. Thiago had taken care of everything, that much he told me as I drove across the country. He started to say something but choked it down. I followed the trail of cigarillo smoke flowing from his open window to the funeral home. My boss called along the way to tell me my presence was no longer needed. I had never been to California or this close to the land of my father.

There were many cars outside when we pulled up, beaters and rides I would never even dream to own, sleek shapes that glowed under the dying sun. Thiago offered me a smoke and we stood for several long moments in silence, watching as men, women, and children entered the funeral home and when we were finished we joined the procession. We weaved through the mourners of another dead love, but following the signs we found the mass was for Rodolfo. We gathered in a large room around the coffin. Most of my days leading up to that moment, looking down at him, I could not remember anything of him, his thick face and callused hands, but I knew, looking down, that he was a mirror for me and Thiago, that we were him in a younger year. Around us were other reflections of our father, his broad nose and black eyes shared. Thiago had known, these new brothers and sisters alien to me, ten of us in total plus the grandchildren and those Rodolfo had defeated at the billiards table.

A gaunt white man in a plain suit walked over to Thiago. The two spoke and it was time. We said our goodbyes to our father's body and followed as he was led to the crematorium. I kissed my fingers and laid them on the smooth coffin, unsure what my heart should contain. The white man pushed the box onto a track that led into the waiting mouth of the furnace. Rodolfo was gone.

The moon kissed the heavens as the column drove to the coast. The sea glittered out in the blackness and we stood at the tide. I took off my shoes and dug my toes down, finding the warmth hidden in the sand. We stood around Thiago as he wept, the urn clasped against his chest as if it were a child. Rodolfo's brother, his face carved with deep wrinkles, held my father's cure, and in broken English said, It was his favorite. A young boy, my nephew, gripped a bottle of mescal. When Thiago lifted the top of the urn, all voices died. He brought a handful of ash and lifted it to the stars. Rodolfo's children did the same. The wind carried our father with our laments out into the sea. We left his cue on the beach. I embraced my brothers and sisters for the first time and then it was only Thiago and I. We tasted the salt on the breeze and he gave me the urn, a small portion of ash still there.

We drove south, past the border and the liquor store where our father died. We went farther, and Thiago told me more stories of Rodolfo, of the town he was born. We drank mescal and talked of staying there forever, playing pool with our father's ashes.

A
MURDER
BALLAD

The body had been lying on the riverbed for only a day when the shepherd found it. He stood above the corpse and spat into the river. He said a prayer and took the goats back to their keep. As he walked to the police station the shepherd ran into the butcher, the only man in the village that he knew by name. The shepherd told the butcher what he had found, about the girl, and the butcher agreed it was best that he tell the police. The shepherd thanked him for his advice and as he entered the police station an old woman with a face coated in dust who overheard the conversation began her job of spreading the news around. Her first stop was the other old women that spent the morning under the shade in front of the church, then to those at the shops. By the time the shepherd lead the police to the body, Ignacio had heard the gossip and was on his way back to the hacienda, his eyes searching the dirt for the words needed.

Ignacio approached Raul as the man sipped his morning coffee. The old mestizo could feel the words hanging unsaid in the vaquero's throat. Raul held the cup to his lips and as he watched Ignacio's mouth tremble with the imitation of words, he was numb to how hot the drink was on his own lips. They found a body, Ignacio said.

Raul asked, Is it her?

That's what they think. Mestizo girl. Long hair. They found her by the river.

Rafael?

No one in the village has seen him for days.

Find him.

Ignacio nodded and swallowed the goose egg that had formed in his throat, wiping his dusty eyes with the back of his hand. He turned and went to the rest of the hands out in the field. Work was called off for the day. Raul sat on the veranda with his coffee and a cigarillo. Whenever his eyes looked to his daughter, they were of velvet, but today they had turned to stone.

When Inez was a girl her father pulled her up onto his horse with him and carried her out to the field where his cattle stood dumb and mute. With one hand he put her on the ground and she walked among the livestock. Her father guided her to a cow and pointed to the beast's flank, to the design burned into the skin and muscle by her father's workers. She ran her fingers over the raised burn like she could find its meaning through touch. That night she dreamed Ignacio and Hector held her down on the dirty ground of the barn as her father pressed a glowing hot iron to the skin of her lower back. Her dream father said that she was no better than the cattle we butcher. Her sheets were soaked when she awoke, running to the bathroom to retch and run her cold fingers over the skin. Inez did not speak to her real father for a week.

Inez was a child of the dirt, spending her time in a concentrated effort to ruin the white dresses Raul, her father, constantly bought in the village for his grief, leaving the dresses soiled and in tatters from playing in the river and the fields or exploring the small stretch of forest to the west of her father's hacienda. Her stepmother, Myra, tried to keep the girl clean but there was nothing the woman could do, no words could tame the girl, nor could Raul's hand stop her games. When Inez's mother died, the girl was young and resisted when Raul moved his mistress into his dead wife's bed, struggled when Myra was made his wife. Inez was always polite to the face but when the back was turned, she would take to undermining the will, anything to prove that

Myra was less of the woman her mother was, that no man should do what her father did. The men of my village are all the same, she thought. The sanctity of marriage is nothing to any of them.

When her father brought home from the village the dress Inez would wear for her Quinceañera, the stepmother demanded the girl put it on so it could be fitted. Inez complied and allowed the woman to make sure it was perfect. The stepmother turned her back for a moment and told Inez to take off the dress, but when she turned back around the girl was gone, having decided to feed the goats. Her favorite, Oro, a beast the color of the tequila her father drank on cool evenings, jumped up and left two hoof prints of mud on the breast of the peach dress. Myra was furious and threatened murder and bloodshed and all Inez did was laugh. When Raul got home Myra went straight to him and talked about the dress that was now ruined, the smile that Inez bore when she showed her stepmother the animal's mark. Raul found Inez playing with Oro like it was a dog and thought of calling over Hector to put the animal down and prepare it as a stew, but when Inez's bouncing eyes caught his, he could but smile. He gave the girl enough love for two daughters. That night he went to the village and bought a new dress for his daughter. Two days later as she prepared for her Quinceañera the breeze carried the scent of rain through the window as she put on her new dress. Raul came to his daughter and told her it was time to become a wife. Inez told her father that she did not want to belong to any man. It doesn't work like that, he said.

In his mind, Rafael laid claim to Inez one Sunday in the year before Inez's Quinceañera. He sat on the pew behind the girl, her father and stepmother. Rafael spent the entire sermon watching her shifting her body on the hard wood seat, brushing her long black hair behind her perfectly-shaped ears. At that age, Rafael only had experience with the poor daughters of the men his own father employed, awkward movements behind their barn late at night, his hands rough on delicate skin, the girls doing anything to make him happy and insure themselves a better life. The things he did with those girls he would never be able to do to Inez. Rafael's father was a man of money and pure blood, while Inez's father was more Indio than Spanish. At such his young age, Rafael knew he would have Inez for his own.

That night he told his father that he was in love and the old man, Javier, laughed, patted the boy on his back and said, One day, my son, you should have her. And Rafael believed him. He had known Inez since they were small, and every chance he got to look upon her, he felt his lust growing, and his need to have her. The boy's mother said nothing. Whenever he saw the girl, Rafael would stand close to her, taking in the nearness, enjoying every moment. He would tease the indio children to get her attention without thought that she herself was mestizo. One day Rafael focused his attention on a little boy named Jacinto. Rafael hit the boy and made fun of how dark his skin was. When Inez heard the words that Rafael said, she walked up to him and, even though he was larger than her, bloodied his nose. Rafael ran home with a smile on his face.

Inez crept into Rafael's dreams but the girl there was not the same one in the waking world. This one was kind and quiet and when he wanted a meal, she would make one and when he wanted to have her she was willing. His was her will, but even though Inez was promised to him, she cared not about bending to his desires.

Two years after her Quinceañera, Inez was engaged.

The marriage was not decided by Inez and Rafael, but by their fathers. Javier came to Raul's hacienda when the girl was seventeen and Javier had the offer to combine their families, their businesses into one. Together, they would be better off than separately, and their lines would continue onward. For a moment the thought came to Raul that if Inez had been born a boy, it would be both his name and his line that would continue. He wanted Inez to be taken care of, and a man of Rafael's station would provide. When Raul agreed that the marriage would take place, that their families would come together, he did not consult with Inez.

They are a family of wealth, Raul said.

So are we.

But not like them, Raul said. Javier was the first man of our village to buy an automobile.

I prefer the horses.

Rafael will take care of you.

Is this your will?

It is.

The two families came together in celebration of the wedding. Javier's table was laden with drink and food and all were gone within hours. When her father and stepfather were busy talking with Rafael's parents, Inez pulled her future husband away into a room that she didn't realize was his bedroom. He smiled like a drunk coyote and pulled her close enough for her to feel his excitement pressed to her, smashing his lips against hers, his hands fumbling like a child over her body. She pushed him back and he fell onto his bed. He smiled dumbly until she held up a finger like a blade. He grew still. I am to be your wife, she said, but that was not my decision. I will fulfill the expectations our parents have of me, but I have expectations of you.

Of course, he said, standing from the bed and stepping close to her until she stopped him with a finger over his heart.

If I am to be yours, then you will be mine. Only mine. If you are to share me with no man, than I will share you with no woman.

Of course, my love.

Good.

She left him there with his excitement.

On the night before her wedding, she dreamed that she stood at the base of a great mountain that scraped at the bellies of clouds. She saw the ocean and the desert and cities where people came together in crowds that stretched from one horizon to the other. She heard songs of foreign lands she could only imagine. She met men completely different than those of her village and she met one who was kind like her father but who lived only for her. When she woke she smiled until she remembered that later that day she would become Rafael's wife.

* * *

Leticia was a girl without a father. She would talk to her dolls of the man she imagined had laid down with her mother and how he was rich and handsome and the nicest man in the village but when she tried to ask her mother questions of this mythical man they fell from her mother's ears and lay dying on the dusty floor of their small home. Her mother sold tortillas in the village square while Leticia went to school. They never wanted for food or clothes. Some nights her mother would give Leticia a small amount of money and tell her to go to the cinema or to the church and not to return for several hours. When Leticia would return home her mother would be flushed and still in bed, her skin like coffee and exposed to the breeze and when Leticia would ask why she had been sent out, her mother said that she needed time alone with the girl's father.

On the evening before the marriage of Inez and Rafael, he went with his friends to the village's bar and they ordered three bottles of tequila and several beers and it was Leticia who brought them their drinks, who caught Rafael's eye. The girl knew nothing of the following day's ceremony and when Rafael smiled at her she felt herself grow warm. He was handsome and she knew he came from the best off family in the village. When he took her hand and led her to the alley behind the bar she didn't fight him. When he kissed her neck and her breasts she smiled. When he was inside her, she felt like a woman, like her mother during those hidden nights with the man who was Leticia's father. The next time they met, Rafael was married but he did not tell Leticia that, he waited for several months, until the girl was in love and she couldn't refuse him anything.

Inez and Leticia, they could have been sisters. Their skin was the same brown and their hair had the same curls. When she stood in the doorway to the room she shared with her husband, watching Rafael curled on the bed with the other woman, Inez could have been watching herself with him. She did not make her presence known. She left the house, then the village. No one there would see her again.

When he was finished, Leticia pressed her face to his bare chest and inhaled. This was the first time they were together in his house. She envied the wife whose bed she lay in. We could be husband and wife, she said. I could be yours.

You are mine, he said.

But you are not mine.

No.

If you leave her, we could be together. We could be real.

I will not leave her.

I could tell her. I see her around the village, shopping or visiting with her father.

Aren't you happy?

You only want me to fuck me. I will tell Inez and we can be together then.

Rafael sat up in the bed and brought his fist against her face. When she started to cry, he told her to shut up. When she refused, he shook her. When his hand went around her throat, she stopped crying. She was still.

When Raul walked down into the cool basement of the police station he held a handkerchief to his nose. The doctor guided him to the clean white linen and pulled it back, exposing the face of the body, the girl with skin darker than most, with curly hair and thick brows. The doctor asked if this was Inez and Raul said no, it was not.

That is good, the doctor said.

I have lost a daughter.

In their bed, Myra pretended to sleep beside Raul, who did not bother with the pretense. His boots were still on his feet and his hat rest like a cat on his chest. With every passing moment, something he had never before felt grew in his heart. A hand knocked on the door and he rose. It was Ignacio. We found him, the vaquero said. Raul turned to Myra, who still held the illusion in her place on the bed. Raul left with his old friend and Myra kept quiet, turning to face the window, her face moist.

Ignacio led Raul to the front of the hacienda where two horses were waiting. They mounted and rode swiftly through the field of sleeping cattle. A wolf and cub stood at the crest of a hill and watched them, then continued on their way to the river.

The two men rode to the end of Raul's property, where the rest of his workers were gathered around a small fire and a figure prone and bloody on the ground. Rafael was face down in the dirt, his breathing shallow. Ignacio had broken something in his chest and each inhalation was a blade slicing through his core. He looked up when he heard the horses' approach. Raul dismounted and stood above the man his daughter had married.

I didn't do it, Rafael said, his voice halting, soft. I promise you, I did not.

Raul said nothing. His eyes were glistening obsidian. He started to turn away, instead sent a boot deep into Rafael's stomach, causing the prostrate body to heaved. Rafael curled like a fetus for protection and spat blood. Raul did not smile. Ignacio took a pistol from his belt and handed it to his employer, his friend. In Raul's hand, the weapon was something holy. He held it to his lips and whispered a prayer to the Christ, the Saints, and his daughter. With his boot he pushed Rafael onto his back. Rafael's lips trembled with a thousand apologies and Raul pulled the trigger, the explosion echoing into the night and dispersing unheard save by those there. The bullet ripped through Rafael's stomach.

It took fifteen minutes for Rafael to die. The ground swallowed his blood and bile and when he was still and quiet, Raul helped his men dig a hole in the dirt.

Inez watched the waves break on the shore as she waited outside the small chapel of Saint Juan de la Cruz. The boat was waiting to take her to a great city, a place where the people stretched from one horizon to the other. When she saw all she could see there, she would find a mountain and sit at its foot and breath deeply. She belonged to no one but herself and that was all she ever wanted for herself.

WHERE
THE WATER
MET THE SKY

Even with years and borders between them, Alvaro always strived to return to her. She was a daughter of the sea, her father a fisherman, as was his father and so on, back through the centuries. They went to the coast to celebrate their marriage, though they could afford little more than a room. She smiled at the way the land became the sea. They found a local who agreed to take them out, to show her what the earth looked like from the ocean, so she could feel what it is like to have only the depths beneath her feet. They went past the horizon, where there was ocean for a mirror of the vault of heaven. The weight of the sky crushed down upon his shoulders, the ocean eager to consume him whole. Alvaro's wife pretended not to see his tears.

Alvaro stood in line for ten minutes to pay his bill. Before the cellular phone, he would stand in line for the same time to purchase the calling cards. It was a ritual more than anything. He bought his calling cards from Josué, a tiny Ecuadorian man who ran the grocery store up the road from him. He paid his phone bill at a mall kiosk across from a stand that sold cups of elote and horchata. It was not so expensive any longer to call back to his home, to his wife and child, but as he gave the clerk his number and paid cash for his monthly allotment of minutes, Alvaro was aware of the growing pointlessness. He worked six days a week and wired money back to his family. He kept enough for his share of the rent and incidentals. To spend on himself was a sin. His clothes came secondhand and he slept on a living room floor. He had not driven since his last stay in the north. A friend had asked for a ride to the bus station. This was when he had gone to Florida for work. The car had been purchased for two thousand dollars in cash, and when the policeman tapped on his window Alvaro knew it was pointless. They put him in detention and he signed whatever papers they put in front of him before putting him on a bus with guards that dropped him off across the border, back home. This would be the first and last time he would return to the place of his birth. He was in that town for two days. Nothing but the clothes on his back, his wallet empty save for his Matrícula Consular and a sheet of paper with the names, addresses, and phone numbers of all the people he knew, wife and child, brothers and cousins. He had to call in favors he never wanted to call in to get enough money wired from his brother, Jorge, who had permanently settled in the north, to get to his family's home in Guanajuato. His wife, Aida, would not answer her phone, nor their son, Alejandro.

The clerk gave him his receipt and a fake smile. Alvaro considered a cup of elote but that would have cost him three dollars and those dollars were better suited for his son's pocket. He had come to the mall with Jorge and his family. They lived in a house within walking distance of the small apartment Alvaro rented with several others of his stripe. Their visits were regular, several times a week, and were always capped off with a request from Jorge for Alvaro to move into his family home, though Alvaro always said no, pride being enough to make a stupid decision. To inconvenience another soul was a sin. Jorge and his family came to the mall to prepare for the arrival of Chava, the third brother. Chava had found a coyote to bring him back north. He last called from El Paso two days before, where he was about to board a bus to bring him to the brother's chosen home in Illinois. He was due in that very night. Alvaro had made the trip twice before. The first time had been fine. He paid and they were men of honor. The second time had been different. It was a hot day when they met him for his last crossing. The coyotes Alvaro paid to take him north picked him up from beside his father's grave. He had not been there for the old man's passing, and could not say if he would be able to be buried in the same dirt as his family. The coyotes put him into a cargo trailer pulled behind a pickup truck. There was nowhere to sit except for the scorching floor. They drove for a day, picking up more crossers as they went until there were nine sweltering in the metallic heat. Each had given money for the privilege with the promise of more once they were safely across. The sweat that dripped from his nose evaporated before it hit the floor. They told Alvaro they would hand him over to some colleagues who would take him on the actual crossing. In the middle of the desert, they stopped the truck and pulled out their knives. A man, his skin burnt dark by age, resisted, and they used the blades on him. The rest acquiesced, and the men with knives left them standing under the noon sun, leaving one man with a gun to watch as they waited in the heat. The heavens stretched out above them like the maw of a god and Alvaro wept. Day turned to night and back again before a pin of light appeared on the horizon. They did not know on what side of the border they were on, all was desert and sky and it could have been people with guns meaning to send them back south or kill them trying. It was another truck, the colleagues to take them on the second leg of the journey. They had plastic milk containers of warm water and it would be three more days before the travelers were able to eat.

When he was a boy he was afraid of the sky. In daylight, it was an ocean suspended above, or Alvaro was hanging, ready to fall into the deep expanse at any moment like a spider dangling above a flame. Once, Alvaro took all of his father's fishhooks and attached them to his shoes, so with each step he would be safe if the earth ever let go of its grasp. When Alvaro's father, Santos, found out, he made the boy bleed. Santos was a hard man, known in their village as a great worker and a strong fighter, but he was as pious as his namesake. He apologized to Alvaro, indirectly as was his way. He said that there was nothing to be feared in the sky, that as it was in the above so it is here below, that we came from up there and one day, if He wills, we would rise to the sky again. This did nothing to alleviate the boy's fear, of course. The sky of the day was one thing, but it was the night that moved him to tears, when the whole of the universe opened up, the vastness of it all revealing to him how little he mattered, how if there was a He up there, surely He couldn't be concerned with a runt of a boy in a small Guanajuato village. Alvaro's grandfather lived almost ninety years and even if he could come close to that lifetime, it would be nothing in the face of time. All traces of Alvaro's blood would be wiped away with the rest of the chalk. It never went away, this fear, but he learned to protect against the fear. Walking through towns and cities and deserts with eyes cast downward, only seeing birds when they tried to steal his crumbs. Clouds became foreign, to say nothing of the stars. He lived on the earth with no thoughts of heaven. His eyes grew murky as time went by and it became harder for him to see. Years after the fishhooks, he met a young woman. She was beautiful, and she became his wife. After they went to the sea, they had a child and Alvaro knew what would have to be done. He paid the coyotes and they took him north.

Jorge found him sitting on a bench across from the kiosk. Alvaro's eyes had taken on a silver tint from the cataracts. Alvaro often found himself lost in his sight, trying to make sense of what used to be plainly shown to him. Jorge nudged his knee to wake him from the self-imposed stupor. Jorge and Paola, his wife, carried bags of clothes for Chava, some they hoped to give to Alvaro though they knew he would never accept them. He took the bags from Paola and they weaved through the crowd back to their car, Alvaro walking two steps behind them. Chava would need work, and that was something Alvaro could provide. His boss would need more workers out in the gardens. The storms would come soon and they would need to clean. The winter prior he worked eighteen-hour days to clear the snow away. When he finally slept his hand was tightly clawed as if he were still holding the shovel. Chava would not like it but he had debts to pay, he had children, Alvaro's nieces and nephews he had never met. It had been five years since he had kissed his own wife, shook his own son's hand.

The terminal was in Chicago. The bus would be there at just past one in the morning. Alvaro would be back at work at seven. For a small moment he considered not going with Jorge to pick up their brother, but to show cowardice is a sin. They drove in silence punctuated by shared yawns. The interstates were clear out in the border towns, but even at such an hour Chicago's streets were a suicide run. Cars he would never dream of owning, cars that cost more than a lifetime of work, sped by like meteors in the night. Jorge lit a cigarette and cracked the window, as Paola had stayed at home with their children. He offered the pack to Alvaro, who accepted and mirrored his brother.

Chava was waiting for them outside the terminal, a backpack hanging from one shoulder, his clothes rumpled from the two-day trip. The whites of his eyes were a dark red, as all the men of their families came to be. They embraced and exchanged their greetings. Alvaro had forgotten how much taller his brother had always been than himself. Chava was asleep before they were back on the highway, waking as they pulled into Jorge's driveway. The three brothers sat in silence as the car cooled in the night, thinking to themselves how long it had been since so much family had been in one place. When an aunt died two years ago, Jorge, who was made legal during the amnesty, had flown home and seen sisters whose names he had forgotten. Alvaro found out about the death weeks later. She had been a favorite of his. Jorge asked his brothers to stay outside for a few minutes while he went in to check on his family, who had been asleep for hours. Chava and Alvaro stood in the awkward silence of the night, each stretching to break away the aches that were their burdens. Alvaro told Chava that he had a job waiting. Hard work, but good pay. Chava smiled, then his eyes went dark. He lit a cigarette and offered one to Alvaro, who declined. Chava asked, When was the last time you spoke to your wife, your family?

It had been longer than he wished. A month. The calls he made that he worked so long to afford went unanswered and unreturned. Despite the money he sent, his wife would have to work, and his son would be at school, and working as well. They were busy. When they sent Chava back south, he had gone to town of their birth, where Alvaro had bought a home he never slept a night in. There is a man living with your wife, your son, Chava said, and Jorge heard this as he came back outside, three bottles of beers in his hands, spitting a low curse. Chava had not wanted to tell this to his brother, older but frailer than himself, and as he watched the light drain from Alvaro's eyes, he regretted it still, but a man needs to know such things.

The next day, Alvaro and Chava rode together to work, their manager having picked them up from Alvaro's apartment as he always did. He showed the work and when they left that night, a day's worth of labor wearing on their backs, Alvaro knew he had worked his last day. When Chava went to sleep, he scribbled a quick note to his brother, leaving the apartment key and enough money to do him well for several weeks. Midnight came and, still weary, he started walking. He took Washington Street for several miles, through poverty and isolated blocks of splendor, past the train station and the dry docks, great boats bigger than homes tucked away from the coming cold. He walked through industrial blight, fields perfect for tending save the chemicals soaked through to the clay. He climbed a fence that blocked off the harbor for the night and went through the sand until he came to the dock, where he had to walk leaning forwards to brace himself against the wind. The lake was a big as the sea he had taken his wife to see so long ago. Part of him wanted to spit at the memory, but it would only blow back in his face. He had broken with his old life crossing to the north, now it was time to break with his current life.

In the desert there was nowhere to hide from the sky. It glared down at the world with hatred and hunger, but here there was more to fear. The very land was poison, picking us off slowly until there were two men, young and old, and me. In the water it was worse. As above so it is below. He was a lone, small blur in the vastness of the world, creation looming large and uncaring around him. He kept rowing, further still, chasing the horizon, hands shaking from the cold and the fear, but he kept moving, because to stop would be a sin.

MORROW

The two boys were out in the woods that day because their father Boyd was not. The summer was inching closer to the end and the boys were trying to milk as much time as they could away from home, away from their old man. The boys were twins, Boyd Jr. and Lucas, but they were not sure who was older and if he even remembered himself, their father never cared to reveal the answer to that secret. Boyd Jr. took an elder's responsibility for Lucas, who took after the mother more and Boyd had never been keen on the resemblance.

When Boyd's truck pulled off from the dirt road earlier than his shift allowed, tossing dust and loose pebbles out behind as it went, they were eating at the kitchen table. Their early morning hours had been spent dragging their father's empty beer bottles, a garbage bag's worth, down to Puckett's Gas and Grocery to get the deposits back, which bought a bottle of Coke and a pack of peanut butter crackers each plus a little extra they split. It'd been the first time they had made the trek, as they would take the bottles through field and hinterland to Morrow Byatt. He lived in a leanto in the woods out by the old Burnett plantation. He hauled chairs and chester drawers from where he found them, nailed paintings into trees and created an imitation of a home in Morrow in his corner of the forest. His best find was a small wood-burning stove found behind Freyer's pub that he used to cook what little meat he caught, mostly squirrel and rabbit. His days were spent gathering up empties and taking them down to Ronny Puckett for change or going down to the Creek to keep away the heat and dirt. His government checks were delivered to his daughter's home in Gastonia but she never delivered the proceeds or took the time for a visit. The boys liked to help out Morrow and Morrow liked to see a pleasant face every now and then. He gladly took cans and gave the boys a couple dollars each, all he had in his pockets to give. He was older than their father, older than Ronny Puckett or Pastor Lawrence at the Presbyterian church, even. Folks around said he had been in the great war, had been there when they let the Jews out of the camps and when he came back he was never quite the same. Maybe three weeks back, the twin's had brought him a nice load of bottles and he paid them as always. The boys waved and said their goodbyes, starting out of the woods, where they would follow the road down to spend their coin at Puckett's, but Morrow stopped them. "Just want you boys to know you can take your bottles down to Puckett's from here on out for yourselves. I'm going to be leaving for a while, might be a spell before I come back. I'll miss seeing you young'uns around." The boys nodded and walked out into the full bright of the sun, neither really thinking on what he said, just craving a cold Coke and maybe something for their stomachs.

Soon as the truck came to a screeching halt in the driveway, Boyd Jr. went to the window for a moment, saw his father's shirt already yellow beneath the arms, around the neck from the day's damp heat. Swaying with each step, his eyes were still like the pond beyond the fish joint up the road, but there was no showing what was happening beneath. Boyd Jr. pushed Lucas out the back door and they ran until they hit the tree line, then they ran some more. Down dead riverbeds and over felled trunks, through tunnels of sweetgum, staghorn and devilwood, cutting across game trails. A doe watched them pass from under the safety of shade. When she no longer heard their hollers or felt the rumble from their steps, she went back to her child, not knowing that in another six months the doe would be the boy's supper. On the night of the solstice, in the quiet hours of full dark Boyd would leave Frayer's, a barn converted into the local beer joint. He would pass the bridge over Long Creek before taking the curve at Hornet's Nest Presbyterian faster than should be necessary, meeting the doe as she crossed. The body would bounce over the hood and spider-web the windshield on impact. "No need to waste meat," he'd said. "If God didn't want us to eat it, he'd have moved her out of the road, or slowed my truck, made me leave the bar earlier or later or anything. Point is," Boyd said, "we got meat."

The boys went deep, past the creek, their flight coming to its conclusion as the boys stumbled out of the brush and into the clearing that surrounded the schoolhouse ruins. Panting and bent crooked, palms on knees, they stayed quiet for a spell, making sure their father was not trouncing on through the woods after them. Little was left after a hundred years but the mud brick chimney and two stone walls, a floor of eroded planks and a bit of ceiling pocked with holes. No glass remained in the frames. There had been no class taught within the rotting walls in near on a century, its students all surely to dust. At one point a road had cut through the woods, coming from town and coming straight up to the door, but nature had taken a claim to it, as it was striving for the building itself.

The boys' breath had run away from them and they stopped to catch it.

"Did he look angry to you?" Lucas said, still hunched over.

Boyd Jr. nodded. His eyes went hard and he absently scanned the woods. A hawk screeched. Squirrels jumped from tree to tree. Beyond that, the forest was static and unstirring.

A thin silver string dipped from the corner of his lips, the end coming to a rest on the forest's dirt floor. "Think he got sent home again?" Pinpoints of sweat formed over his forehead.

"Don't know. Might have not been no more work for him today," Boyd Jr. said before he went and sat with his back against the one of the walls, enjoying the coolness that spread through his skin. The building's remnants groaned at the inconvenience but held. He tried not to think.

"I don't want to go back home tonight." Lucas walked over and borrowed his brother's posture.

"You never do." Boyd Jr. would not say as much, but held a similar desire.

"We can catch some fish and eat supper out here tonight."

Boyd Jr. replied, "There ain't no fish in that creek. Maybe frogs, snakes, but no fish," but his words came from a mind elsewhere.

"I ain't going to eat no frogs," Lucas said before he spat to show his distaste.

"The French do it all the time. I even heard they had a taste for guinea pigs, too."

Lucas sneered but did not respond. They sat there as the sun inched its way on home, the sky a bright blue but a claret darkness was creeping up to the west. The blackbirds' songs slowly rising in desperation. A coyote called out to its kin on the wind that cut through the leaves above still that were on their slow fade to death and rot.

"Want to go and see if Morrow's come back yet?" Boyd Jr. asked, to which Lucas nodded, a smile spreading across his lips. They stood and stretched, then made their way past the derelict schoolhouse, through hill cane and gray dogwood then deeper, going beneath shagbark and bluejack, braiding around poison ivy and dodging snake holes. They came out on McCoy Road and cut across, through Lawrence's untended field, barren since the old man could not so much as leave his bed anymore. Stalks left to decompose where they stood as offerings to the crows. They followed a trail cut from the road and around the field, hugging close to a forest of green ash. Morrow's leanto was at the other end of the field, past the monument put up for the men and women who tended the land when it was the plantation, four foot high and made of stone with words of apologies fashioned into the surface. The old-timers who spent their days sitting in the shade outside of Puckett's, spitting tobacco juice to join with the dust, would weave words about the wooden grave markers out in these woods, slave cemeteries entrusted to the shadows of trees and bones dragged up by plows, shaded specters that held on to the anger of their disrupted rest. Lucas held his breath as long as he could as they walked on, until bright sparks danced before his eyes, trying to trade silence for safe passage. Boyd Jr. kept his eyes on what passed for the trail, picking out the perfect place to land his steps, knowing Lucas would follow him perfectly.

They cut through the quiet of the tree's shelter, until the forest opened up at Morrow's home. Boyd Jr. was glad his body shielded his brother's line of sight. Morrow's home there formed by a sheet of scrap tin at a fat angle against the base of a black oak that kept his bed dry. The stove that took him two days to drag here through the forest, the old man not even thinking to move his squat to match the find, was still there in the midst of the detritus collected over an indigent lifetime. Sitting a short distance off in the chair that always gave a small bit of comfort to the man, sat what remained of Morrow Byatt. He had been in the chair for weeks, perhaps he had sat down there once the boys left and he never rose again. Morrow was out in the wild long enough for the muscles to loosen and the skin the weaken, for animals take bits of him away. There was nothing above the man's neck, and looking over the leaves that coated the floor of his makeshift home they could see no sign of his head. The boys had liked him despite the smears of dirt across his face and clothes, the stench that built between his bi-weekly baths in the creek. He spoke to them honestly and held back nothing from the things he had seen in his days walking through life, and all he had wanted was someone to know he wouldn't be around much longer.

After a moment pregnant with a mourning neither boy had ever the need to practice, Boyd Jr. tugged at Lucas' hand, and they retraced their steps, back through the field, across road and creek, through wood and past their home, where inside their father snored on the kitchen floor. They walked back up to Puckett's as the light of day finally died, looking for someone to tell that Morrow was not around any more.

CASTLE

The board we used was older than me by decade, near on two. Basic, the pieces were carved from walnut. Some were kept together by wood glue, some by duct tape, like the box itself, the folding board gone near yellow in places. Most days he won, some days the victor was me. Rarely. The old man was good, great. I never had the mind for it, to be honest. Never grasped thinking four, five moves ahead. He just smiled that sly smile of his, the one you rarely saw, when he found his opening. This was what we did on holidays. Go down to the garage as they all talked upstairs. One year, can't quite say when, we just stopped playing. Maybe I got too old, too bored with those gatherings that I'd cut them short as possible. I think he won the last game. Maybe he'd say it was me. But just to play him, I'd say the opposite, whether or not my king survived.

ABOUT THE AUTHOR:

Chris Deal is from North Carolina. His debut collection of short fiction, Cienfuegos, was originally published by Brown Paper Publishing and was later reprinted by Kuboa Press. His work has been featured in the anthologies *Warmed and Bound*, *Booked*, *you're dead and I killed you*, and in various other places. He currently resides in Illinois with his wife.

ACKNOWLEDGEMENTS:

I've never been one to talk about myself. Luckily, here I can talk about other people, those who helped me so much along the way, in ways small and large that, really, they themselves probably don't realize. To Pela Via for pushing me to write the best stories I'll ever be luckily enough to put down on paper, and for thinking I can do better. Richard Thomas, who is an inspiration to be around. Jesse Lawrence, for knowing where the best blood is. Sean Ferguson, for knowing the best poop jokes. JR Harlan, the mighty. Livius Nedin and Robb Olson for telling me what to read. Amanda Gowin, Nik Korpon, Bob Pastorella, Rob Parker, Caleb Ross, Gordon Highland, Drew McCoy, Gavin Pate, Michael Gonzalez, Craig Wallwork, Eddy Rathke, and the entirety of the Velvet for giving me a home. Sallie for letting me use her word processor when I was a kid, Clint for showing me what it was to be man, and for every damn thing else. Nancy for being there for me now. J. David Osborne for letting me be a part of the best damn collection of writers, and for believing in these stories. To everyone I forgot.